UNWIN HYMAN SHORT STORIES

IT'S NOW OR NEVER

INCLUDING FOLLOW ON ACTIVITIES

EDITED BY JANE LEGGETT

AND ROY BLATCHFORD

Unwin Hyman Short Stories
Openings edited by Roy Blatchford
Round Two edited by Roy Blatchford
School's OK edited by Josie Karavasil and Roy Blatchford
Stepping Out edited by Jane Leggett
That'll Be The Day edited by Roy Blatchford
Sweet and Sour edited by Gervase Phinn
Pigs is Pigs edited by Trevor Millum
Dreams and Resolutions edited by Roy Blatchford

Unwin Hyman Collections
Free As I Know edited by Beverley Naidoo
Solid Ground edited by Jane Leggett and Sue Libovitch
In Our Image edited by Andrew Goodwyn

Unwin Hyman Plays
Stage Write edited by Gervase Phinn

This edition 1992 by
CollinsEducational
77–85 Fulham Palace Road
Hammersmith, London W6 8JB

First published 1985 by Unwin Hyman Ltd

Reprinted 1987, 1988, 1990

British Library Cataloguing in Publication Data

It's now or never – Unwin Hyman Short Stories
  1. Short stories, English   2. English fiction –
20th century
I Leggett, Jane   II Blatchford, Roy
823'.01'08 [FS]   PR1309.55

  ISBN 0 00 322292 6

Typeset by Typecast Limited, Tonbridge
Printed and bound in Great Britain by Billing & Sons Ltd. Worcester

Series cover design by Iain Lanyon
Cover illustration by Chris Burke

Contents

Introduction

Fiction has always been a major resource for teachers and students involved in the study of language and literature. Perhaps its most important contribution has been the enjoyment and pleasure that readers gain. Equally, fiction has been used because of its power to engage attention and the imagination, and give shape to personal experiences and expectations.

Many of the issues we wish to discuss with older students are complex, challenging and probing. Reading fiction provides a chance to consider and reflect on them from a distance, before moving into the realm of personal experience and opinion. Fiction also offers a wealth of models of writing and expression that can be used to assist students in their own writing.

The aim of this collection is to provide a resource for 16–19 year-old students following a course which includes a study of language or literature. This may be within a sixth-form or a college, pursuing a variety of pre-vocational and academic courses.

The stories have been selected first and foremost because they are fine examples of the short story genre, and are perhaps best enjoyed when read aloud and shared with a group of students. But they also offer opportunities to talk and write about issues that are of concern and relevance to this age group. The stories have been loosely arranged around certain themes so that ideas and issues encountered in one can be linked with another (see page 128 for details), but there is no necessity to move chronologically through the volume.

Opening the collection is 'Pin Money', a powerful tale focusing on women and men in the workplace and what happens when unemployment threatens. Two of the stories — 'A Dangerous Influence' and 'True Romance' — are uncompromising and challenging accounts of personal relationships and are likely to provoke considerable discussion and feeling amongst students. 'Samphire', 'Sumitra' and 'The Story of an Hour' might be read alongside each other as studies of tensions within and about marriage, while 'Meeting in Milkmarket' and 'Happy Birthday' offer moving, at times funny, 'slices of life' revolving around themes of friendship and childhood. In striking contrast, 'The Sniper' is a poignant tale set in war-torn Ireland and highlights the deep personal and family tragedy of civil war.

'Sumitra', 'Reunion' and 'Coffee for the Road', in very different ways, examine cultural conflict and racial tensions, and are guaranteed to engage students in debate about their own personal feelings and experiences. 'White Lies' is related in theme though injecting an element of macabre humour, while 'Nineteen Fifty-Five' is a compelling and beautifully crafted tale centring on the world of music and youth culture. 'A Lot to Learn' is included as a rare and brilliant example of the *short* short story, which students may wish to emulate in their own writing.

The range of 'Follow On' activities is designed to present a variety of talking and writing assignments that will help students to gain in confidence and competence at using language effectively in any context. More specifically, the activities aim to encourage students to:

- ▶ work independently and collaboratively
- ▶ consider:
  - — the short story as a genre
  - — language and style of a writer
  - — structure and development of plot
  - — development of character
  - — setting
- ▶ examine the writer's viewpoint and intentions
- ▶ respond critically and imaginatively to the stories, orally and in writing
- ▶ read a variety of texts, including quite difficult ones
- ▶ read more widely

Many of the stories are followed by authors' comments specially written for this collection, and these can provide fascinating perspectives on the genesis and meaning of the tales.

One important footnote: the activities are divided under three broad headings — *Before, During* and *After Reading*. The intention is that students should engage with the text as closely as possible, from predicting storylines to analysing characters' motivations. Teachers and lecturers using the collection are therefore recommended to preview the 'Follow On' section before reading the stories with students.

In compiling this volume we have made particular efforts to bring to students both women and men writers, and stories which have female and male protagonists. We are also grateful to students we have taught for their comments on many of the stories in *It's Now or Never.*

Jane Leggett   Roy Blatchford

JENNIFER GUBB

Pin Money

The latch on the front gate was frozen to the hasp and Tracey's fingers stuck to the iron as she fumbled with it. She stood in the road waiting for the factory bus and the cold seeped through her clothes and twisted into her bones like a blade. Half past six on a cold dark January morning. She shivered. She wished the bus would come. In the silence she could hear it throbbing, still parked in the square, the engine idling. Doris again. The second time this week.

The hard iciness of the road spread through the soles of her shoes. She stamped her feet, hearing the resonance of metal-tipped heels striking stone. Bloody Doris. They should leave her behind. The engine noise changed. Gears crashed. She heard the bus whining towards her. At the corner the driver changed down, then he changed down again on the hill. The same sounds every morning. The same people, the same day ahead. Only the time of the sunrise was different.

Headlights, the sound of bushes swishing along the sides of the bus in the narrow lane. White letters leapt out. Potatos — Free Range Eggs, Swedes. Tracey's father had left out the 'e' in potatoes when he painted the sign on the tin shed. Hissing air brakes. Clanking door.

' 'Lo, Tracey'

'Morning, Tracey'

'Tracey'

' 'Lo'

Laconic early morning greetings. The bus was warm, fuggy.
The windows misted over, the air thick with the first cigarette
smoke. Tracey sat in her usual seat against the warm solid bulk of
Winnie, twenty years her senior. Sometimes she cried about
Winnie. Twenty years packing dead chickens. She'd worked at
the packing station since she was fourteen, cooped up for eight
hours every day in the stench of raw blood and new-killed flesh
and burning feathers. The smell nauseated Tracey each morning
as they drove through the gates. Winnie had seen some changes
though. They used to kill the birds with a thick stick and a carving
knife, cheerfully moving up and down the lines. Now the lines
moved, a continual lurching chain of squawking chickens passing the electric stunner. Patient men and women stood in the
same spot day after day slitting throats, chopping heads, wings,
feet. In the old days they'd sat on chairs around a tin bath
overflowing with feathers, old sack bags for aprons, talking,
smoking, laughing as they plucked the hens. Now a flailing,
hissing steam machine did the job. Talking was impossible.
Hygiene regulations said no fags. Everyone stood all day, it was
more efficient. They all wore white net scarves over their hair,
green nylon overalls, white rubber boots. It was warm though.

In the old days they'd frozen. Dreadful chilblains they got. And
rheumatism. They'd had to wear thick coats which made their
arms ache as they plucked. Now they had showers and central
heating and piped music. It was much better these days, Winnie
said. But they didn't have the laughs the same, somehow.

Idly, Tracey listened to the conversation around her.

'Bloody cold waiting there, Tracey.'

'Mm.'

'Doris couldn't get out again.'

'If I'd got an old man like her's, I wouldn't be able to get out
fast enough.' Laughter.

'I 'ates this job in the winter. Is it ever worth it, when you could
'ave a lie in?'

'I'd rather do this than ask my 'usband for money — 'ee wants
to know 'ow every penny's spent.'

'It's not bad — apart from getting up. I mean it's not heavy
work.'

'Gives you a bit of independence like.'

'Pays for the bingo and a few little luxuries. I got a Teasmade now — it's lovely these mornings. Nice hot cup of tea when you're still all cosy in bed.'

'We couldn't manage if it wasn't for my bit. 'E don't bring much 'ome out of 'is pay packet. Spends more in the pub dinner-time than I gets for all the week for me 'ouse keeping.'

'I never tells my old man what my bottom line is, else 'e'd keep more of 'is.'

Tracey could smell the stench now as they drew up to the factory gates. Nearly half past seven. They'd have to run if they were to get their boots and overalls and hair nets on, to clock in on time. They docked a quarter hour if you were late. Around the gate stood a shuffling bunch of men, disconsolate, ill-humoured. There were a few extra ones today. For months they had gathered there each morning for the vacancies list to be posted. It made the women uneasy to see them there — resentful, humiliated, out of work. Sometimes one of the men would shout a bitter insult at them, or thump angrily on the side of the bus as it passed amongst them through the factory entrance.

In the old days the men hadn't wanted to work on the line, the pay was low and the work monotonous. They had stuck together in jobs that were manly, jobs where they fought for high wages and better conditions. The chicken factory was women's work, it paid pin money. There were a few men there, in management or doing the killing, but they got paid on a different rate. They didn't have to launder their own overalls either. But now when jobs were short the men sang a different tune, they wanted the women to make way for them.

'More of 'em today', said Winnie, jerking her head in the direction of the gate. Nobody answered. In the cloakroom it was a mad scramble to change into their uniforms. They clustered around the clocking-in machine, trying to get all the cards through before the hands reached half-past. They trooped into the packing shed and stood in their places. When they were all in position, Winnie signalled to the man in the glass-fronted office above them and the line started. Tracey held her plastic bag open ready for her first chicken of the day. It was always hard for the first half hour, her fingers were stiff and cold and it took her a while to get into the swing of it. Violet and Connie pulled out the innards, Gert and Laura chopped off the heads and feet, Mary and Maggie folded back the wings, trussed the birds and popped the giblets back inside, Tracey and Doris packed the chickens into bags and Winnie weighed and labelled each one. Elsie went up and down the line with a big bin on wheels. Her job was to clear up the innards and to salvage the giblets for Mary and Maggie. Poor chickens, Tracey thought, alive one minute and having another chicken's giblets stuffed into them the next. A burst of pop music broke in on her thoughts. Violet and Connie speeded up in time with the beat, the chickens came thick and fast, there was no time for anything except total concentration on the task in hand.

'Pick up yer chickens!' Winnie called out, throwing two chickens she had missed, back to her. Feverishly she rammed them into bags, desperately trying to catch up with herself. She had a little pile of chickens on the bench beside her now and she couldn't seem to reduce their number. Doris leaned across and took some from her, working faster than ever, her hands like lightning. Finally the pile had gone and she could work at a more human rate. She looked across at Doris and mouthed through the crashing machine noise.

'Bloody radio.' They always switched it on when the line slowed to less than a hundred chickens an hour; it made them work faster. At last it was ten o'clock. The line stopped with a shudder. They took the cotton wool out of their ears and gathered around the tea urn. Today there was a letter for each of them with their cake and tea. It was from the management. They had had a directive from central government to offer voluntary redundancy terms to all married women workers. The letter pointed out how generous the terms were, a week's untaxed wages for every year worked paid direct through the Department of Health and Social Security on production of a P.45. The last paragraph had had an emotional appeal. It exhorted the married women workers to think of the unemployed men who languished jobless and depressed throughout the length and breadth of Britain. It asked them whether it was just, that some privileged families should receive two wages while others had none.

'Bloody cheek', said Winnie, who had four children and whose husband worked in the killing shed. 'We couldn't manage on Jack's wages.'

'Why don't they send it to married men as well, if they reckon there should only be one wage going home — what does it matter whose wage it is?'

'Not many families could live on a woman's wage, love.'

'But if one of *us* goes, they're only going to get a woman's wage. They'd be better off on the dole.'

The bell rang. They drank down their tea and drifted back to their places. The morning dragged, they wanted to talk but instead they were locked into their own minds by the clattering conveyor belt and the blaring pop music. They worked grimly, anxiously, until dinner time came.

Over their sandwiches in the canteen, Violet and Connie announced that they were going to accept redundancy. Thirty years mounted up, they said. Violet could have a new three piece suite and Connie wanted a deep freeze.

'Sounds a lot,' said Winnie, 'but it won't last long.'

'Better to hang onto your job.'

'But it's true what they say,' said Connie, 'I'm doing a bloke out of a job. It's not right.'

'Why should a bloke work instead of a woman then?'

'A bloke needs a job. They get ever so down when they're out of work. A woman's got plenty to occupy her but a man wouldn't know what to do with himself stuck at 'ome all day.'

'Why couldn't he do all the things around the house?'

'Wouldn't be right, would it. You can't expect them to cook and clean, the same as a woman would.'

Connie and Violet were adamant. They'd had enough of the factory. It would be nice to stay at home, to lie in a bit, to go around to one another's house, to get their husband's tea ready before he got home instead of rushing around when he was there, trying to do it all quickly before he started grumbling. Most of the women prepared the meal the night before so that they only had to light the gas when they got home. And they could spend their mornings shopping, instead of dashing out in their lunch times each day. The others were doubtful, but they could see the appeal. Any one of them would have taken a golden handshake if they could. But the rest of them had no choice. Tracey had to pay her mum her lodge, anyway she'd only been there two years. Doris's husband was out of work himself. Winnie couldn't afford to give up because her oldest two were going to college now and their grants didn't go far, and in the holidays they ate so much. Mary had bought a lot of stuff on the knock so she needed every penny to keep up the payments. Maggie lived on her own and her widow's pension hardly covered the rent. Elsie, who was a bit backward, lived with her ageing father, a cantankerous man who made her life a misery. She liked coming to work because it got her out of the house, provided some company. None of them liked the job, but it was better than no job at all.

Violet and Connie signed their forms and went up the stairs to the office to give in their notice. The other women envied them their choice. But they felt uneasy, betrayed perhaps.

Mary said, 'Well I'm not giving up my job for no bugger. I've lived all me life with second-hand furniture and jumble clothes. I want me own stuff now, new. Not sofas that other people have farted in.'

'This is just the start', said Winnie. 'Voluntary redundancies. Next it'll be all the married women who've got husbands with a job. And then it will be you single girls. They'll say you don't need so much money as a bloke — like they do now, that's why they don't pay a decent wage for women's work. You mark my words. That's what's coming. They're trying to get us all out.'

Two weeks later Violet and Connie were replaced by Fred and Sid. They got paid more than the women, thanks to the special subsidy the government introduced for every male worker, they got round the Equal Pay Act by re-defining the job. Fred and Sid had to look out for blemishes on the chicken's skin as they pulled out the innards and for this they received a bonus.

The women were incensed. They complained bitterly to the supervisor. But he only shrugged, 'It's all part of this government incentive scheme to get blokes off the dole queues. It's better for the company to take on men now — and you can't pay them women's wages can you? It'd be less than they got in benefits. They wouldn't work for it.' Fred and Sid kept themselves to themselves. They were very slow so the women had an easier time of it. No amount of music could speed Fred and Sid and the target rate had to be put down to eighty-five chickens an hour. It gave the women more time to think. And they thought. They thought mainly about Fred and Sid and the men clamouring for jobs at the factory gates each morning. There was a tension, an antagonism between them and the men. They brooded about the injustice that they saw, and their resentment hardened into a determination not to be ousted. In the tea breaks, they sat apart from the men. Outwardly they were no different. They knitted, they filled in crosswords, they read glossy women's magazines just as they had always done. But beneath the umbrella of these activities they were talking; the idle chatter of earlier days took on a new significance and they reached out together for the changing patterns, the unforeseen links, the unexpected directions that gradually became apparent to them. A casual eavesdropper could not have detected the change, and the women themselves could not have said that there was any difference. But the emphasis had shifted, ever so slightly, ever so subtly, and yet enough to make them sit apart, to make them suspicious, to make them take refuge in each other's company. They exchanged comments, not aiming them at anyone in particular, just dropping them into the pool of conversation, like pebbles, so that they lay there intricately cobbled amongst them all.

They were not prepared for Elsie's letter when it came, but they had been forecasting something of the kind so they were not taken entirely unawares. Elsie couldn't read, so Tracey read the letter aloud in the group as they crowded around the tea trolley. It was a dismissal note. The management had declared that Elsie was incompetent, unfit for her work. Elsie's fat, round face crumpled, the tears rolled heavily down her cheeks. She blubbered through her sniffling distress, 'But I do's me job alright. They never complained before. I do's it alright, don't I Winnie?'

'Course you do Elsie, you do's a good job, nobody could do it better.'

Her weeping became a wail of despair as the full meaning of her dismissal dawned on her.

'I don't want to say 'ome with 'im all day. I likes coming in 'ere with all you girls.'

She looked around at them all, helplessly, appealing to them for help. Tracey thought of Elsie's dad, ancient, bitter, complaining. They said he used to interfere with Elsie, that's why she was a bit doolally. Poor old Else. She'd hate it, stuck there with her father, day after day.

'Don't you worry, Else. We'll stick up for you. We'll go to the union', said Winnie.

At dinner time, the women told the men what had happened

and asked Jack, Winnie's husband, to call a union meeting. The men grumbled and shifted uncomfortably, irritated that their card game had been interrupted.

'All a fuss over nothing,'

'It'll blow over,'

'Don't get your knickers in a twist — there's no need for a union meeting.'

'I'll have a word with Mr Holdsworth this afternoon, see if we can't sort something out.'

The meeting in the afternoon was unproductive. Jack could see Mr Holdsworth's point of view. After all, Elsie was a bit half-witted, a man could do her job in half the time. The women turned on him, openly hostile, angry, shouting.

'She's worked here all her life.'

'She does her job alright.'

'It's just that they're trying to get rid of the women.'

'They want to put a man in so they get this government subsidy.'

'And you buggers are all for it.'

This last remark provoked the men to retaliate.

'She isn't all there.'

'It's just charity, giving her a job.'

'What does she want money for? — she only spends it on her bloody cats.'

'There's all those blokes out there, outside the gates with families to support — what about them?'

'She should stay 'ome and look after her father, poor old sod, 'e can't do anything for 'imself.'

The women retreated. The arguments were all true. The whole weight of established opinion, of commonsense was on the side of the men, of Mr Holdsworth, of government. The men felt a responsibility as bread winners, it was natural that they should have first choice of any paid work going. Mr Holdsworth had to keep his profits up or there would be no jobs for anybody, he couldn't afford to ignore the government subsidies, it was in the interests of the whole community to accept them and all that went along with it. The government saw that the national economy was a cake of a finite size, it was in the interest of all citizens that the cake should be divided equitably they said, and the obvious unit for consuming each slice was the family. It was neat and efficient and cost effective to have men earning in the labour market and women managing the domestic scene. It was part of the natural order, it was supported by thousands of years of tradition, it was stated categorically in the Bible. Besides, men without paid work are disruptive. And anyway, Elsie wasn't quite all there.

They went back to their knitting and their magazines and their crosswords. And the muttering began again. Carefully, slowly, they built up a new picture, a picture which did not match the one that the men had painted for them. It was a picture where Elsie stood, massive and intense in the foreground. Behind her were the machines and the institutions that housed them. The women concentrated their attention on Elsie. The machines and the institutions did not interest them, they were not important; they ignored them. The men should have listened to their conversation, it was mild and gentle and parochial, but there was a thin line of sharpened, tempered steel stretched through it.

'Elsie's under the doctor.'

'How long before she's worked her notice?'

'Another three days.'

'She'll 'ate being at 'ome.'

'What will she do with 'erself all day?'

'Oh 'e'll 'ave her running around him from morning 'til night, you wait.'

'They say he used to interfere with 'er.'

' 'E's got arthritis now, all crippled up.'

' 'E led 'er mum a dance when 'e was younger. She used to be black and blue Sundays.'

'Elsie won't be able to stick it — she'll crack up.'

'Or kill 'im more like.'

'She'll 'ave to 'ave all they cats put down.'

'Costs a lot to keep a cat nowadays.'

'And she won't be able to take 'ome a bag of innards for them every night, like she's used to.'

'Won't be able to afford Bingo night either.'

'She do love the Bingo, too.'

'It's a shame.'

'Funny old girl, she is though. What about Friday's? Always goes off with 'er sandwiches, down to the killing shed, to watch Jack stick the pigs.'

'Don't know how she could stomach it.'

'She says she likes the noise. Makes her tingle.'

'Well, she won't be tingling no more.'

'What'll 'appen to 'er?'

'She'll go down hill.'

'It's not very clean up there now. Council bloke's bin on at 'er about they cats.'

'It'll get worse if she gets fed up.'

'She'll 'ave to be careful they don't put 'er away.'

' 'Eart of gold though, old Else.'

'Do anything for anybody.'

'No 'arm in 'er at all.'

'Won't be the same without 'er. She's bin 'ere all the time I can remember.'

As they talked, they fuelled their determination to keep Elsie amongst them. The prospect of her impoverishment, if her dismissal went through, was too much for any of them to contemplate. Imperceptibly they formed a resolve. They would not abandon her to the perilous slope of destitution and misery that their imaginations had conjured up for her. They would gather round her, protect her, shield her, keep the ravening prospect at bay.

Only one man noticed the quiet purpose amongst the women. He was Arthur. His wife was a paraplegic. Arthur shared with the women the knowledge of the joyless sprint to the shops at lunch-times, the lost wages on the frustrating day at home waiting for the gas men to call, the busy Saturdays bustling with urgent trivial tasks — prescriptions to collect, rooms to be cleaned, sheets to be laundered.

'I don't know if there's anything I can do', he said shyly, diffidently, 'but I'm on Elsie's side. If they can get rid of her that easily, they can get rid of all of us.'

In the cloakroom as the women prettied their hair and painted their mouths and powdered their faces, the talk was fiercer.

'The next thing will be that you can't work if you're married and your husband's got a job.'

'They'll say he's got to support you, like they say down the Benefits office, when you try to get your dole.'

'Even when you pay your stamps they won't let you have it.'

'Then it'll be the single girls. They'll say you're your father's responsibility, 'til you get a man of your own.'

'Or they'll give you a training course and a bit of pocket money.'

'Or they'll pay child benefit to your mum and dad 'til you get married.'

'They keep 'aving these programmes on the telly now, about how you can save a lot by staying at home and making do and mending.'

'But you would 'ave to ask your old man for money every time you wanted some extra.'

'Bugger that.'

'My old man's never 'it me, not since I got this job. 'E knows I'd be up and gone if 'e did, cos I've got me own money now.'

'Yeah, that's all I come 'ere for, the money and to see me mates and 'ave a laugh. They can stick their job right where I stick the giblets.'

Back on the line, they were especially friendly to Elsie as she passed them, picking up the tatters of raw flesh and the trailing gizzards that sometimes got left behind. They grinned at her, winked, shouted over the noise of the machinery, bumped against her as she bent near them. They wanted her to know that they were with her. And all the time they were mulling things over, waiting for the next tea break to swap their private thoughts.

'Funny how none of the men wanted these jobs before.'

'Not enough money.'

'Too hard.'

'Too dirty.'

'You can't skive when you're on the line.'

'Why can't they stay at home and draw the dole — there's always something in a house they could be doing.'

'They don't like being on their own.'

'There's nobody to 'ave a laugh with.'

'They think it's women's work at 'ome.'

'They've changed their minds then.'

'Well, I don't see why they should 'ave Elsie's job, 'coz they've changed their bloody minds, all of a sudden.'

'Nor do I.'

Some of the women looked angry. Some of them talked with feverish indignation. Tracey's eyes and cheeks were glowing with excitement. Only Winnie stayed silent. She was the oldest, the most respected, their tacitly elected leader.

'What shall we do, Win?'

It was the question that they had been preparing for. A hush fell as they waited for her reply.

'We've tried the union. We've tried a deputation. To my mind it's no good striking — they'd just sack us all and give our jobs to the men. It'd be better for old Holdsworth, then he could get his bloody government subsidy. And you can be damn sure the men wouldn't support us.'

'What else can we do then?'

' 'Ave a sit in.'

'What's that?'

'Lock ourselves in the office where the machine button is. They can't do anything if the machines are switched off. Just stay there 'till they give Elsie 'er job back.'

No one answered. None of them had ever done anything deliberately defiant. They were reasonable women, kind-hearted. They just wanted a quiet life, they were not law breakers; they instilled the traditional values of truth and care and kindness in their children. An act of open rebellion was a violation of their closely cherished beliefs. There were murmurs of doubt, dissent.

'What else then? Anybody got a better idea? It's Elsie this week but it could be any one of us next.'

They were agitated. Back on the line they snapped at Fred and Sid.

'Clean out these bloody chickens.'

'This is the fifth one in a row with its gizzard still in.'

'Send 'em down regular, not in bunches.'

'This one's got a broken leg, send it back up.'

Doris dropped her plastic bags in a slithering row across the wet floor. Tracey's back hurt and she kicked the pallet away and stood on the wet concrete instead so that her feet got cold. Mary was irritated by the way Maggie sniffed. Winnie put the wrong weight labels on the chickens and the supervisor came down to check her scales.

On the way home in the bus they planned. Blankets, food, coffee, knitting, books. Winnie agreed to 'phone Arthur, to ask him to stand by in case they needed him. Tracey promised to write a leaflet for him to read out to the press. The rattling bus muffled their quiet voices, the men sitting in a row in the back seat dozing, smoking, talking, saw nothing unusual in the murmur of sounds. There was an air of importance about the women as they said goodnight, and a set about their bodies as if they were physically squaring up to their responsibilities.

The group of men clustering around the factory gates next morning was larger than usual. News of Elsie's dismissal had got around. It was a cold dreary morning and they were disgruntled and dispirited, frustrated to see so many others like themselves, hopeless, aimless. There was an ugly scuffle as the bus arrived.

'Go home and look after your bloody kids.'

The bus was thumped and bashed by the fists of the surging irritable crowd. The women were shaken, guilty, until Winnie said, 'What makes them think they've got a God-given bloody right to 'ave our jobs?'

The demonstration of resentment against them only made them more determined to make their stand over Elsie. All day there was an air of suppressed anxiety, time and again a woman had to be replaced by the supervisor while she went to the lavatory.

'I don't know what's the matter with you lot today — must've been eating dandelions.'

At 5.15 they hurried off to the cloakroom as usual. Tracey stayed behind to talk to Wilfred who was in charge of locking up. She watched carefully to see that all the office workers had left and then, just after Wilfred locked the main door and they had set off together across the tarmac of the bus park she said, 'Oh, I left my purse and house keys by the line. Give us the keys Wilf and I'll nip back and get them.'

'You'd forget your head if it wasn't screwed on', he grumbled.

The other women were waiting by the door. Quickly they slipped inside and Tracey locked the door behind them. They set about building barricades. The bus driver hooted impatiently and then Wilfred and some of the men came back to see what was happening. There was a blaze of light from every window in the building.

'Tracey, Tracey', Wilfred sounded angry.

'Go on home, Wilfred, we've locked ourselves in.'

'We're staying 'ere.'

'You can't do anything about it.'

'We're not coming out 'til Elsie gets her job back.'

Wilfred looked frightened, he was directly responsible to Mr Holdsworth for security in the factory, he had failed in his duty by letting Tracey take the keys. The keys should never have left his possession at any time. The other men began calling out to the women, one of them was Jack, Winnie's husband, 'Winnie are you in there? Winnie you get out 'ere now or it'll be the worse for you.'

'Come out, you silly buggers.'

'What good do you think it'll do?'

'You're mad.'

Some of the unemployed men who hung around at the gates, now joined them.

'We got families. She didn't have nobody to look after.'

'We got a right to jobs too.'

They rattled on the door, shoved at it with their shoulders in their frustration with the women.

'Winnie are you coming out or not?'

Jack's voice had a warning, a threat in it. Winnie was pale, but remained silent.

'Winnie!' He paused for a reply.

'I'll break this bloody door down, mind!'

Wilfred intervened, and put a hand on his arm, 'You can't do that Jack, it's company property'.

'It's my bloody missus in there. What about the kid's tea? WINNIE!'

The driver of the bus hooted again.

'Come on!' he yelled, 'I've got the pictures run to do at half past six.'

The men hesitated. Wilfred said, 'Come on, I'll deal with this. I'll get on the phone to Holdsworth. You lot go home.'

They shifted awkwardly, muttering, pushing back their caps in indecision, shrugging their hands deeper into their pockets. They milled about for a few minutes more and then gradually drifted off to the bus.

'Come on, Jack. There's no point hanging around here.'

On the bus, they sat in the front seats, leaning forward into the aisle, elbows on knees, hands dangling loose.

'Cutting off their noses to spite their face.'

'It won't get them anywhere.'

'Holdsworth won't give in.'

'Just puts everybody's backs up.'

'Pissing in their own bed sheets.'

'They should 'ave done it through the union. Followed procedure.'

'They 'aven't got a leg to stand on, what with Elsie being simple.'

'They should 'ave got rid of her years ago.'

'They'll come off worse.'

Inside the factory, the women stood about wondering what to do next now that the hectic activity of barricading themselves inside was completed. It was silent and odd, with the line still, the rows of pallets on the floor, the empty conveyor belt, the naked bodies of the chickens hanging head down from their hooks ready for tomorrow's start. If there ever was a tomorrow's start again. The floor was spattered with blood and bits of flesh. Contract cleaners came to the factory at 6 each morning.

'We'd better clean it up here, I suppose. We can't eat our tea in all this muck.'

They were glad to be doing something. They set to with a will, cleaning, sweeping, brushing down the puddles under the pallets, scooting the water and bits of flesh along the gutters to the big drains in the corner, wiping down the machines with disinfectant. When they had finished they put all the mops and buckets and cloths back into the cleaner's cupboard, which was underneath the stairs that led up to the glass-fronted office overlooking the factory floor.

'Where shall we eat our tea?'

'There's nowhere to sit comfortable.'

'We could go up to the office.'

There was an awed silence. The office was hallowed ground. None of them ever went there. If there was a query about wages, or a wound that required first aid, the office girls came down to them. Winnie rallied them.

'Come on. We can't stand up all night — this is supposed to be a sit-in. We've got to park our bums somewhere.'

They climbed the stairs. Tracey tried several keys from Wilf's bunch before she found the right one. They marched in, like an occupying army. Each settled herself at a desk.

'Take a letter, Miss Jones.'

'Mr Holdsworth, I'm afraid we're going to have to give you your cards.'

'Lovely, comfy chairs.'

'I've always wanted to spin round in one of these.'

'Girly magazines! This must be Mr Parker's desk. Dirty old man.'

They unpacked their Thermos flasks and sandwiches and cleared a space on their desks. They were excited and jolly, like schoolgirls at a party. Raucous, vulgar, ribald. Then the phone rang. It silenced them suddenly; no one wanted to answer. Winnie was the leader by unspoken consent, she picked up the receiver. It was Mr Holdsworth, she mouthed the name to the others, her hand over the mouthpiece.

'Yes.'

'Yes, it's true.'

'No we won't.'

'We're not leaving until Elsie gets her job back.'

Winnie was firm. There was a loud chattering. She held the phone away from her ear so that the others could hear the tirade. The effect was comical. Tracey mimed winding-up a gramophone. The others encouraged Winnie.

'You tell 'im Win.'

'Don't take no notice of 'im.'

'Hang up on 'im.'

Suddenly they felt powerful, united in a just cause, fighting for Elsie. Nothing else mattered.

'We're stopping here until Elsie gets her job back,' Winnie repeated, 'that's all there is to it', and she put the phone down with a bang.

'He says he's coming round here with the police.'

'Let 'im.'

'They'll have to break in then.'

'We're in the right over Elsie.'

'We better check that all the windows are locked.'

'We can take the phones off the hook and shut the office door and we'll be as snug as anything.'

'We won't even 'ear 'em cos this place is sound-proofed against the noise of the line.'

Tracey found the radio panel and after a few minutes of experiment, Radio 1 burst out, echoing through the empty factory, bright, cheerful incongruous music shattering the darkness and striking against the deaf ears of the dead chickens.

Tracey began to bop, fingers clicking, eyes closed, shoulders shaking. Doris got out her knitting. She could get a lot more done here than at home, there were no interruptions. Winnie did the crossword. The others settled for a game of whist. Tracey suddenly disappeared down the stairs and into the factory, reappearing a few minutes later with one of the birds.

'First prize. A chicken dinner', she announced, banging it down, cold and stiff and angular on the improvised card table.

'Cosy in'it, really', observed Doris.

Outside police cars gathered. Mr Holdsworth stormed up and down; pleas were made through loudspeakers, threats, quotations from the law, appeals to common sense. But the women cocooned in the soundproof office, bathed in the blare of pop music, spent the evening quietly ignoring the commotion. They could guess what was happening from the blue circling lights on the ceiling and the occasional loudspeaker announcement that penetrated, but they chose not to respond. By midnight the furore had died down. One police car remained parked at the factory gates. They settled down for a night of fitful sleep, some lying on the floor, others propped up in their chairs, their feet resting on the open desk drawers.

Next morning they turned the radio to the local station and listened to news of their sit-in.

'. . . unfair dismissal . . . barricaded themselves in . . . a spokesman for the company said . . . union officials will go to the factory this morning . . . admitted to a policy of employing men rather than women to comply with the spirit of recent government legislation . . .'

'There! That's what it's all about.'

'Unfit for work! That was just an excuse.'

'They'll get rid of us all as soon as they can think up a good enough reason.'

Through a loudspeaker they heard Mr Holdsworth.

'. . . futile action . . . company is adamant . . . breaking the law . . . those involved will be dismissed . . . small minority of militant agitators . . . no official union support.'

The women listened and commented.

'Bugger the law. It wasn't written to help people like us.'

'Militant agitators! US! US! he called us militant agitators!'

'Course the union won't support us — they never do when it's women. We wouldn't even 'ave a vote, if we'd 'ad to wait for them.'

Then the union official hailed them.

'... go to the central committee ... set up arbitration ... investigate complaints ... co-operate with union ... thrash out an acceptable solution ... management is threatening to lock out the other workers, to deprive them of their wages ... We appeal to you, think of your brothers!'

All day they remained stubbornly inside. They telephoned an account of the grievance to Arthur so that he could contact the local radio and newspapers. Tracey read out a statement of their demands through the open window, to the knot of people gathered in front of the factory. They could see Mr Holdsworth, and Jack, and Sid and some of the unemployed men who congregated each morning by the gates, standing in a huddle around the union official. A policeman sat in his panda car. At lunch time they listened to the news programme and heard their local M.P. talking about the problem of unemployment.

'... a man's sense of purpose ... his dignity ... to support his family ... working man all his life ... suddenly deprived of his identity ... statistics show that more men suffer from depression ...'

That night they settled once more to sleep, there was a bond between the women that had not existed so strongly before. For a whole day they had listened to arguments and produced between them counter arguments. They saw clearly how they were regarded as dispensable units in the labour market, to be adopted or discarded at will. They sympathised with the men. But they needed the work too. The shared understanding brought strength and a binding sense of purpose. They felt a warmth and affection for each other that the grinding relentless work on the line had obscured from them before. They joked as they prepared for their second night's vigil.

'Mind I don't cock me leg over you, Doris, in me sleep.'

'I had more sleep last night than I ever get with Harry. He's a terror for it.'

'You're lucky. It has to be me birthday before my old man'll perform.'

'I always find myself looking at the clock, wondering how much longer.'

'Yeah it's better to get it over with early, or else you're not fit for anything the next day.'

'I used to like it more. But gets boring after a few years.'

'Wouldn't say no to Gregory Peck though.'

'Yeah, make a change anyway.'

'He's probably in a wheel chair by now.'

Gradually they fell asleep. The silence was profound. Even the radio was quiet now. A grunt, a movement, a scuffle of twitching limbs were the only sounds in that great empty factory, with its chains and cogs and grinding belts lying idle.

Outside a group of men gathered. Some were men from the factory and a few were recognisable as men who crowded around the vacancies board every morning. They wore woollen hats and dark overcoats. They carried iron bars and thick sticks. The police, huddled in their car at the gates, dozed to the sound of late night radio music.

There was an earsplitting crash as the door caved in, running footsteps on the stairs and a sound of splintering glass as the men burst into the office. The women had no time to protect themselves.

In the brief moment of clarity before the stick crashed down on her head, Winnie saw that her attacker was Jack.

Writing this short story was like embroidering a picture. The background was the general one of unemployment in Britain in the 1980s. In the middle distance was a conversation I chanced to hear on the radio when an unemployed man complained bitterly that married women were taking all the jobs. In the foreground, in bold relief, was an experience I had of working in a chicken-packing station when I was seventeen. I put the whole thing into a political perspective that had begun to develop at the end of my first week in that factory when I found out that the boy who had been working next to me on the line had earned £14 and I had only earned £8. It was before the Equal Pay Act. All the threads then got worked into the fabric of the story and the title presented itself to me last of all. — Jennifer Gubb

ALICE WALKER

Nineteen Fifty-Five

1955

The car is a brandnew red Thunderbird convertible, and it's passed the house more than once. It slows down real slow now, and stops at the curb. An older gentleman dressed like a Baptist deacon gets out on the side near the house, and a young fellow who looks about sixteen gets out on the driver's side. They are white, and I wonder what in the world they doing in this neighborhood.

Well, I say to J. T., put your shirt on, anyway, and let me clean these glasses offa the table.

We had been watching the ballgame on TV. I wasn't actually watching, I was sort of daydreaming, with my foots up in J.T.'s lap.

I seen 'em coming on up the walk, brisk, like they coming to sell something, and then they rung the bell, and J. T. declined to put on a shirt but instead disappeared into the bedroom where the other television is. I turned down the one in the living room; I figured I'd be rid of these two double quick and J. T. could come back out again.

Are you Gracie Mae Still? asked the old guy, when I opened the door and put my hand on the lock inside the screen.

And I don't need to buy a thing, said I.

28

What makes you think we're sellin'? he asks, in that hearty Southern way that makes my eyeballs ache.

Well, one way or another and they're inside the house and the first thing the young fellow does is raise the TV a couple of decibels. He's about five feet nine, sort of womanish looking, with real dark white skin and a red pouting mouth. His hair is black and curly and he looks like a Loosianna creole.

About one of your songs, says the deacon. He is maybe sixty, with white hair and beard, white silk shirt, black linen suit, black tie and black shoes. His cold gray eyes look like they're sweating.

One of my songs?

Traynor here just *loves* your songs. Don't you, Traynor? He nudges Traynor with his elbow. Traynor blinks, says something I can't catch in a pitch I don't register.

The boy learned to sing and dance livin' round you people out in the country. Practically cut his teeth on you.

Traynor looks up at me and bites his thumbnail.

I laugh.

Well, one way or another they leave with my agreement that they can record one of my songs. The deacon writes me a check for five hundred dollars, the boy grunts his awareness of the transaction, and I am laughing all over myself by the time I rejoin J. T.

Just as I am snuggling down beside him though I hear the front door bell going off again.

Forgit his hat? asks J. T.

I hope not, I say.

The deacon stands there leaning on the door frame and once again I'm thinking of those sweaty-looking eyeballs of his. I wonder if sweat makes your eyeballs pink because his are sure pink. Pink and gray and it strikes me that nobody I'd care to know is behind them.

I forgot one little thing, he says pleasantly. I forgot to tell you Traynor and I would like to buy up all of those records you made of the song. I tell you we sure do love it.

Well, love it or not, I'm not so stupid as to let them do that without making 'em pay. So I says, Well, that's gonna cost you. Because, really, that song never did sell all that good, so I was glad they was going to buy it up. But on the other hand, them two listening to my song by themselves, and nobody else getting to hear me sing it, give me a pause.

Well, one way or another the deacon showed me where I would come out ahead on any deal he had proposed so far. Didn't I give you five hundred dollars? he asked. What white man — and don't even need to mention colored — would give you more? We buy up all your records of that particular song: first, you git royalties. Let me ask you, how much you sell that song for in the first place? Fifty dollars? A hundred, I say. And no royalties from it yet, right? Right. Well, when we buy up all of them records you gonna git royalties. And that's gonna make all them race record shops sit up and take notice of Gracie Mae Still. And they gonna push all them other records of yourn they got. And you no doubt will become one of the big name colored recording artists. And then we can offer you another five hundred dollars for letting us do all this for you. And by God you'll be sittin' pretty! You can go out and buy you the kind of outfit a star should have. Plenty sequins and yards of red satin.

I had done unlocked the screen when I saw I could get some more money out of him. Now I held it wide open while he squeezed through the opening between me and the door. He whipped out another piece of paper and I signed it.

He sort of trotted out to the car and slid in beside Traynor, whose head was back against the seat. They swung around in a u-turn in front of the house and then they was gone.

J. T. was putting his shirt on when I got back to the bedroom. Yankees beat the Orioles 10–6, he said. I believe I'll drive out to Paschal's pond and go fishing. Wanta go?

While I was putting on my pants J. T. was holding the two checks.

I'm real proud of a woman that can make cash money without leavin' home, he said. And I said *Umph*. Because we met on the road with me singing in first one little low-life jook after another, making ten dollars a night for myself if I was lucky, and sometimes bringin' home nothing but my life. And J. T. just loved them times. The way I was fast and flashy and always on the go from one town to another. He loved the way my singin' made the dirt farmers cry like babies and the womens shout Honey, hush! But that's mens. They loves any style to which you can get 'em accustomed.

1956

My little grandbaby called me one night on the phone: Little Mama, Little Mama, there's a white man on the television singing one of your songs! Turn on channel 5.

Lord, if it wasn't Traynor. Still looking half asleep from the neck up, but kind of awake in a nasty way from the waist down. He wasn't doing too bad with my song either, but it wasn't just the song the people in the audience was screeching and screaming over, it was that nasty little jerk he was doing from the waist down.

Well, Lord have mercy, I said, listening to him. If I'da closed my eyes, it could have been me. He had followed every turning of my voice, side streets, avenues, red lights, train crossings and all. It gave me a chill.

Everywhere I went I heard Traynor singing my song, and all the little white girls just eating it up. I never had so many ponytails switched across my line of vision in my life. They was so *proud*. He was a *genius*.

Well, all that year I was trying to lose weight anyway and that and high blood pressure and sugar kept me pretty well occupied. Traynor had made a smash from a song of mine, I still had seven hundred dollars of the original one thousand dollars in the bank, and I felt if I could just bring my weight down, life would be sweet.

1957

I lost ten pounds in 1956. That's what I give myself for Christmas. And J. T. and me and the children and their friends and grandkids of all description had just finished dinner — over which I had put on nine and a half of my lost ten — when who should appear at the front door but Traynor. Little Mama, Little Mama! It's that white man who sings . . . . The children didn't call it my song anymore. Nobody did. It was funny how that happened. Traynor and the deacon had bought up all my records, true, but on his record he had put 'written by Gracie Mae Still.' But that was just another name on the label, like 'produced by Apex Records'.

On the TV he was inclined to dress like the deacon told him. But now he looked presentable.

Merry Christmas, said he.

And same to you, Son.

I don't know why I called him Son. Well, one way or another they're all our sons. The only requirement is that they be younger than us. But then again, Traynor seemed to be aging by the minute.

You looks tired, I said. Come on in and have a glass of Christmas cheer.

J. T. ain't never in his life been able to act decent to a white man he wasn't working for, but he poured Traynor a glass of bourbon and water, then he took all the children and grandkids and friends and whatnot out to the den. After while I heard Traynor's voice singing the song, coming from the stereo console. It was just the kind of Christmas present my kids would consider cute.

I looked at Traynor, complicit. But he looked like it was the last thing in the world he wanted to hear. His head was pitched forward over his lap, his hands holding his glass and his elbows on his knees.

I done sung that song seem like a million times this year, he said. I sung it on the Grand Ole Opry, I sung it on the Ed Sullivan show. I sung it on Mike Douglas, I sung it at the Cotton Bowl, the Orange Bowl. I sung it at Festivals. I sung it at Fairs. I sung it overseas in Rome, Italy, and once in a submarine *underseas*. I've sung it and sung it, and I'm making forty thousand dollars a day offa it, and you know what, I don't have the faintest notion what that song means.

Whatchumean, what do it mean? It mean what it says. All I could think was: These suckers is making forty thousand a *day* offa my song and now they gonna come back and try to swindle me out of the original thousand.

It's just a song, I said. Cagey. When you fool around with a lot of no count mens you sing a bunch of 'em. I shrugged.

Oh, he said. Well. He started brightening up. I just come by to tell you I think you are a great singer.

He didn't blush, saying that. Just said it straight out.

And I brought you a little Christmas present too. Now you take this little box and you hold it until I drive off. Then you take it outside under that first streetlight back up the street aways in front of that green house. Then you open the box and see . . . Well, just *see*.

What had come over this boy, I wondered, holding the box. I looked out the window in time to see another white man come up and get in the car with him and then two more cars full of white mens start out behind him. They was all in long black cars that looked like a funeral procession.

Little Mama, Little Mama, what it is? One of my grandkids come running up and started pulling at the box. It was wrapped in gay Christmas paper — the thick, rich kind that it's hard to picture folks making just to throw away.

J. T. and the rest of the crowd followed me out the house, up the street to the streetlight and in front of the green house. Nothing was there but somebody's gold-grilled white Cadillac. Brandnew and most distracting. We got to looking at it so till I almost forgot the little box in my hand. While the others were busy making 'miration I carefully took off the paper and ribbon and folded them up and put them in my pants pocket. What should I see but a pair of genuine solid gold caddy keys.

Dangling the keys in front of everybody's nose, I unlocked the caddy, motioned for J. T. to git in on the other side, and us didn't come back home for two days.

1960

Well, the boy was sure nuff famous by now. He was still a mite shy of twenty but already they was calling him the Emperor of Rock and Roll.

Then what should happen but the draft.

Well, says J. T. There goes all this Emperor of Rock and Roll business.

But even in the army the womens was on him like white on rice. We watched it on the News.

Dear Gracie Mae [he wrote from Germany],

How you? Fine I hope as this leaves me doing real well. Before I come in the army I was gaining a lot of weight and gitting jittery from making all them dumb movies. But now I exercise and eat right and get plenty of rest. I'm more awake than I been in ten years.

I wonder if you are writing any more songs?

Sincerely,
Traynor

I wrote him back:

Dear Son,

We is all fine in the Lord's good grace and hope this finds you the same. J. T. and me be out all times of the day and night in that car you give me — which you know you didn't have to do. Oh, and I do appreciate the mink and the new self-cleaning oven. But if you send anymore stuff to eat from Germany I'm going to have to open up a store in the neighborhood just to get rid of it. Really, we have more than enough of everything. The Lord is good to us and we don't know Want.

Glad to here you is well and gitting your right rest. There ain't nothing like exercising to help that along. J. T. and me work some part of every day that we don't go fishing in the garden.

Well, so long Soldier.

Sincerely,
Gracie Mae

He wrote:

Dear Gracie Mae,

I hope you and J. T. like that automatic power tiller I had one of the stores back home send you. I went through a mountain of catalogs looking for it — I wanted something that even a woman could use.

I've been thinking about writing some songs of my own but every time I finish one it don't seem to be about nothing I've actually lived myself. My agent keeps sending me other people's songs but they just sound mooney. I can hardly git through 'em without gagging.

Everybody still loves that song of yours. They ask me all the time what do I think it means, really. I mean, they want to know just what I want to know. Where out of your life did it come from?

Sincerely,
Traynor

1968

I didn't see the boy for seven years. No. Eight. Because just about everybody was dead when I saw him again. Malcolm X, King, the president and his brother, and even J. T. J. T. died of a head cold. It just settled in his head like a block of ice, he said, and nothing we did moved it until one day he just leaned out the bed and died.

His good friend Horace helped me put him away, and then about a year later Horace and me started going together. We was sitting out on the front porch swing one summer night, dusk-dark, and I saw this great procession of lights winding to a stop.

Holy Toledo! said Horace. (He's got a real sexy voice like Ray Charles.) Look *at* it. He meant the long line of flashy cars and the white men in white summer suits jumping out on the drivers' sides and standing at attention. With wings they could pass for angels, with hoods they could be the Klan.

Traynor comes waddling up the walk.

And suddenly I know what it is he could pass for. An Arab like the ones you see in storybooks. Plump and soft and with never a care about weight. Because with so much money, who cares? Traynor is almost dressed like someone from a storybook too. He has on, I swear, about ten necklaces. Two sets of bracelets on his arms, at least one ring on every finger, and some kind of shining buckles on his shoes, so that when he walks you get quite a few twinkling lights.

Gracie Mae, he says, coming up to give me a hug. J. T.

I explain that J. T. passed. That this is Horace.

Horace, he says, puzzled but polite, sort of rocking back on his heels, Horace.

That's it for Horace. He goes in the house and don't come back.

Looks like you and me is gained a few, I say.

He laughs. The first time I ever heard him laugh. It don't sound much like a laugh and I can't swear that it's better than no laugh a'tall.

He's gitting fat for sure, but he's still slim compared to me. I'll never see three hundred pounds again and I've just about said (excuse me) fuck it. I got to thinking about it one day an' I thought: aside from the fact that they say it's unhealthy, my fat ain't never been no trouble. Mens always have loved me. My kids ain't never complained. Plus they's fat. And fat like I is I looks distinguished. You see me coming and know somebody's *there*.

Gracie Mae, he says, I've come with a personal invitation to you to my house tomorrow for dinner. He laughed. What did it sound like? I couldn't place it. See them men out there? he asked me. I'm sick and tired of eating with them. They don't never have nothing to talk about. That's why I eat so much. But if you come to dinner tomorrow we can talk about the old days. You can tell me about that farm I bought you.

I sold it, I said.

You did?

Yeah, I said, I did. Just cause I said I liked to exercise by working in a garden didn't mean I wanted five hundred acres! Anyhow, I'm a city girl now. Raised in the country it's true. Dirt poor — the whole bit — but that's all behind me now.

Oh well, he said, I didn't mean to offend you.

We sat a few minutes listening to the crickets.

Then he said: You wrote that song while you was still on the farm, didn't you, or was it right after you left?

You had somebody spying on me? I asked.

You and Bessie Smith got into a fight over it once, he said.

You *is* been spying on me!

But I don't know what the fight was about, he said. Just like I don't know what happened to your second husband. Your first one died in the Texas electric chair. Did you know that? Your third one beat you up, stole your touring costumes and your car and retired with a chorine to Tuskegee. He laughed. He's still there.

I had been mad, but suddenly I calmed down. Traynor was talking very dreamily. It was dark but seems like I could tell his eyes weren't right. It was like some*thing* was sitting there talking to me but not necessarily with a person behind it.

You gave up on marrying and seem happier for it. He laughed again. I married but it never went like it was supposed to. I never could squeeze any of my own life either into it or out of it. It was like singing somebody else's record. I copied the way it was sposed to be *exactly* but I never had a clue what marriage meant.

I bought her a diamond ring big as your fist. I bought her clothes. I built her a mansion. But right away she didn't want the boys to stay there. Said they smoked up the bottom floor. Hell, there were *five* floors.

No need to grieve, I said. No need to. Plenty more where she come from.

He perked up. That's part of what that song means, ain't it? No need to grieve. Whatever it is, there's plenty more down the line.

I never really believed that way back when I wrote that song, I said. It was all bluffing then. The trick is to live long enough to put your young bluffs to use. Now if I was to sing that song today I'd tear it up. 'Cause I done lived long enough to know it's *true*. Them words could hold me up.

I ain't lived that long, he said.

Look like you on your way, I said. I don't know why, but the boy seemed to need some encouraging. And I don't know, seem like one way or another you talk to rich white folks and you end up reassuring *them*. But what the hell, by now I feel something for the boy. I wouldn't be in his bed all alone in the middle of the night for nothing. Couldn't be nothing worse than being famous the world over for something you don't even understand. That's what I tried to tell Bessie. She wanted that same song. Overheard me practicing it one day, said, with her hands on her hips: Gracie Mae, I'ma sing your song tonight. I *likes* it.

Your lips be too swole to sing, I said. She was mean and she was strong, but I trounced her.

Ain't you famous enough with your own stuff? I said. Leave mine alone. Later on, she thanked me. By then she was Miss Bessie Smith to the World, and I was still Miss Gracie Mae Nobody from Notasulga.

The next day all these limousines arrived to pick me up. Five cars and twelve bodyguards. Horace picked that morning to start painting the kitchen.

Don't paint the kitchen, fool, I said. The only reason that dumb boy of ours is going to show me his mansion is because he intends to present us with a new house.

What you gonna do with it? he asked me, standing there in his shirtsleeves stirring the paint.

Sell it. Give it to the children. Live in it on weekends. It don't matter what I do. He sure don't care.

Horace just stood there shaking his head. Mama you sure looks *good*, he says. Wake me up when you git back.

Fool, I say, and pat my wig in front of the mirror.

The boy's house is something else. First you come to this mountain, and then you commence to drive and drive up this road that's lined with magnolias. Do magnolias grow on mountains? I was wondering. And you come to lakes and you come to ponds and you come to deer and you come up on some sheep. And I figure these two is sposed to represent England and Wales. Or something out of Europe. And you just keep on coming to stuff. And it's all pretty. Only the man driving my car don't look at nothing but the road. Fool. And then *finally*, after all this time, you begin to go up the driveway. And there's more magnolias — only they're not in such good shape. It's sort of cool up this high and I don't think they're gonna make it. And then I see this building that looks like if it had a name it would be The Tara Hotel. Columns and steps and outdoor chandeliers and rocking chairs. Rocking chairs? Well, and there's the boy on the steps dressed in a dark green satin jacket like you see folks wearing on TV late at night, and he looks sort of like a fat dracula with all that house rising behind him, and standing beside him there's this little white vision of loveliness that he introduces as his wife.

He's nervous when he introduces us and he says to her: This is Gracie Mae Still, I want you to know me. I mean . . . and she gives him a look that would fry meat.

Won't you come in, Gracie Mae, she says, and that's the last I see of her.

He fishes around for something to say or do and decides to escort me to the kitchen. We go through the entry and the parlor and the breakfast room and the dining room and the servants' passage and finally get there. The first thing I notice is that, altogether, there are five stoves. He looks about to introduce me to one.

Wait a minute, I say. Kitchens don't do nothing for me. Let's go sit on the front porch.

Well, we hike back and we sit in the rocking chairs rocking until dinner.

Gracie Mae, he says down the table, taking a piece of fried chicken from the woman standing over him, I got a little surprise for you.

It's a house, ain't it? I ask, spearing a chitlin.

You're getting *spoiled*, he says. And the way he says *spoiled* sounds funny. He slurs it. It sounds like his tongue is too thick for his mouth. Just that quick he's finished the chicken and is now eating chitlins *and* a pork chop. *Me* spoiled, I'm thinking.

I already got a house. Horace is right this minute painting the kitchen. I bought that house. My kids feel comfortable in that house.

But this one I bought you is just like mine. Only a little smaller.

I still don't need no house. And anyway who would clean it?

He looks surprised.

Really, I think, some peoples advance *so* slowly.

I hadn't thought of that. But what the hell, I'll get you somebody to live in.

I don't want other folks living 'round me. Makes me nervous.

You *don't?* It *do?*

What I want to wake up and see folks I don't even know for?

He just sits there downtable staring at me. Some of that feeling is in the song, ain't it? Not the words, the *feeling*. What I want to wake up and see folks I don't even know for? But I see twenty folks a day I don't even know, including my wife.

This food wouldn't be bad to wake up to though, I said. The boy had found the genius of corn bread.

He looked at me real hard. He laughed. Short. They want what you got but they don't want you. They want what I got only it ain't mine. That's what makes 'em so hungry for me when I sing. They getting the flavor of something but they ain't getting the thing itself. They like a pack of hound dogs trying to gobble up a scent.

You talking 'bout your fans?

Right. Right. He says.

Don't worry 'bout your fans, I say. They don't know their asses from a hole in the ground. I doubt there's a honest one in the bunch.

That's the point. Dammit, that's the point! He hits the table with his fist. It's so solid it don't even quiver. You need a honest audience! You can't have folks that's just gonna lie right back to you.

Yeah, I say, it was small compared to yours, but I had one. It would have been worth my life to try to sing 'em somebody else's stuff that I didn't know nothing about.

He must have pressed a buzzer under the table. One of his flunkies zombies up.

Git Johnny Carson, he says.

On the phone? asks the zombie.

On the phone, says Traynor, what you think I mean, git him offa the front porch? Move your ass.

So two weeks later we's on the Johnny Carson show.

Traynor is all corseted down nice and looks a little bit fat but mostly good. And all the women that grew up on him and my song squeal and squeal. Traynor says: The lady who wrote my first hit record is here with us tonight, and she's agreed to sing it for all of us, just like she sung it forty-five years ago. Ladies and Gentlemen, the great Gracie Mae Still!

Well, I had tried to lose a couple of pounds my own self, but failing that I had me a very big dress made. So I sort of rolls over next to Traynor, who is dwarfted by me, so that when he puts his arm around back of me to try to hug me it looks funny to the audience and they laugh.

I can see this pisses him off. But I smile out there at 'em. Imagine squealing for twenty years and not knowing why you're squealing? No more sense of endings and beginnings than hogs.

It don't matter, Son, I say. Don't fret none over me.

I commence to sing. And I sound — wonderful. Being able to sing good ain't all about having a good singing voice a'tall. A good singing voice helps. But when you come up in the Hard Shell Baptist church like I did you understand early that the fellow that sings is the singer. Them that waits for programs and arrangements and letters from home is just good voices occupying body space.

So there I am singing my own song, my own way. And I give it all I got and enjoy every minute of it. When I finish Traynor is standing up clapping and clapping and beaming at first me and then the audience like I'm his mama for true. The audience claps politely for about two seconds.

Traynor looks disgusted.

He comes over and tries to hug me again. The audience laughs.

Johnny Carson looks at us like we both weird.

Traynor is mad as hell. He's supposed to sing something called a love ballad. But instead he takes the mike, turns to me and says: Now see if my imitation still holds up. He goes into the same song, *our* song, I think, looking out at his flaky audience. And he sings it just the way he always did. My voice, my tone, my inflection, everything. But he forgets a couple of lines. Even before he's finished the matronly squeals begin.

He sits down next to me looking whipped.

It don't matter, Son, I say, patting his hand. You don't even know those people. Try to make the people you know happy.

Is that in the song? he asks.

Maybe. I say.

1977

For a few years I hear from him, then nothing. But trying to lose weight takes all the attention I got to spare. I finally faced up to the fact that my fat is the hurt I don't admit, not even to myself, and that I been trying to bury it from the day I was born. But also when you git real old, to tell the truth, it ain't as pleasant. It gits lumpy and slack. Yuck. So one day i said to Horace, I'ma git this shit offa me.

And he fell in with the program like he always try to do and Lord such a procession of salads and cottage cheese and fruit juice!

One night I dreamed Traynor had split up with his fifteenth wife. He said: *You meet 'em for no reason. You date 'em for no reason. You marry 'em for no reason. I do it all but I swear it's just like somebody else doing it. I feel like I can't remember Life.*

The boy's in trouble, I said to Horace.

You've always said that, he said.

I have?

Yeah. You always said he looked asleep. You can't sleep through life if you wants to live it.

You not such a fool after all, I said, pushing myself up with my cane and hobbling over to where he was. Let me sit down on your lap, I said, while this salad I ate takes effect.

In the morning we heard Traynor was dead. Some said fat, some said heart, some said alcohol, some said drugs. One of the children called from Detroit. Them dumb fans of his is on a crying rampage, she said. You just ought to turn on the t.v.

But I didn't want to see 'em. They was crying and crying and didn't even know what they was crying for. One day this is going to be a pitiful country, I thought.

I wanted to write something about the exploitation of black people's music by white performers and white-owned record companies. Something that reflected the violation and often powerlessness the black musicians feel and the emptiness and sense of artistic poverty the white musicians (sometimes) feel. But I had no idea this story was coming.

I had brooded over the subject for years.

Then one day I lay down for a nap, and the next thing I knew, Gracie Mae was whispering this story in my ear. She taught me a different notion of power — and of pity.

When I finished the story, I knew I need not worry so much about the theft of black people's music; that we will continue to create it because music is one of our most revered connections to, and expressions of, life. The very attempt to steal something so sacred will always lead either to greater self-awareness and a kind of enlightenment, or to simple but devastating confusion. Sometimes, as with Traynor, it will lead to both.

— Alice Walker

LUCY WHITMAN

A Dangerous Influence

Miss Christie always made a point of coming in to take her coffee break with the rest of the staff, unless she was really terribly busy or had to go to a meeting. It was the only time in the day when the whole department gathered together in one room — the tiny common room they had managed to save for themselves against quite considerable pressure from outside.

Today she was feeling rather tired, and was quite glad to stop thinking about her work for the time being and sink into her special armchair by the window, while Marcia, her secretary, a capable, matronly woman who had a grown-up family, poured her out some coffee. Miss Christie accepted the offering with a gracious smile. She did not feel inclined to talk this morning, so instead she just sat there, very upright, and listened to the others. There were two conversations going on.

Marcia was talking about some of the plants she had seen on a recent visit to Kew. The typists, Sandra and Sue, were discussing the men in the other departments. Miss Dangerfield, who was Miss Christie's deputy, entered the room at this moment, and made her way over to the coffee table singing softly to herself, as she quite often did. It was a sort of merry nervous habit that she had.

'Have you seen that skinny one — Clive Andrews?' Sandra was asking.

'Do you mean the one who's dyed his hair bright red?' replied Sue.

'He's turned queer!' said Sandra with a giggle.

This was news to Sue. 'What, *literally?*'

Miss Dangerfield's spoon screeched in her cup as she stirred her coffee.

The new assistant, Lizzie, didn't seem to be making any attempt to join in the fun with the others. She was gnawing at a nail, and barely concealing a scowl. Miss Christie hoped this was not a sign of ill temper, but decided to give her the benefit of the doubt and put it down to shyness.

Marcia, meanwhile, was reaching the climax of her narrative, and everyone present turned their attention to her.

'And you'll never guess what I saw! It was in the Orchid House, there were hardly any people about, and there were these two ladies, quite elderly, you know, and very respectable-looking, very well-dressed. And all of a sudden one of them whipped out a pair of scissors, snipped off a cutting and popped it into her bag, all in a matter of seconds! Can you imagine!' Her audience looked suitably shocked and amused. 'I couldn't believe my eyes, they just whipped out the scissors, took a snip and there we are! And to think, I've often wished I could have cuttings from those wonderful plants, but I wouldn't dream of doing that. And there were these two spinsters . . .'

There was a burst of laughter from everyone in the room, and Marcia skidded to a halt, clapping her hand over her mouth.

'I'm sure that whether or not they were spinsters had nothing to do with it,' laughed Miss Christie.

Marcia was blushing. As it happened, she was the only married woman in the room. All the others therefore were technically spinsters, though probably only Miss Christie, at fifty-nine, Miss Dangerfield, at forty-eight, and Gloria Jones, who was only thirty-four but whose workmates had long ago decided that she had 'had it', would have fitted the bill in Marcia's mind. The others were all young and marriageable.

But none of the three displayed the least inkling of annoyance or hurt feelings. Everyone just seemed to think it was screamingly funny.

Lizzie, new to this particular office, couldn't help being impressed by the good humour which dispelled the awkwardness so fast. She was only going to do this job for a few months, while someone else was on maternity leave. It made a change to work for a woman boss, in a department staffed entirely by women. So far she had not really had any dealings with Miss Christie, but she found her rather daunting. She was very fragile-looking, paper thin and wispy haired, with very formal manners and an almost ludicrously upper-class accent such as Lizzie thought had died out long ago. Today she was wearing a blot of apricot coloured lipstick and a dash of blue eyeshadow, which seemed somehow inappropriate. Her eyes were rather watery, expressing a mixture of wistfulness and severity. She was a stickler for detail, insisting on signing personally all correspondence from the whole department. She alway kept strictly to the prescribed rules and regulations. The women who worked for her all obviously respected her, and Lizzie could not imagine anyone daring to challenge her authority.

It seemed that she had a very cordial relationship with Miss Dangerfield, whose office was joined to her own by an interconnecting door, which they frequently left ajar. Miss Dangerfield was a friendly woman with smiling blue eyes and fair wavy hair. She had a full figure, and wore very well-cut clothes. Lizzie found her much easier to get on with than Miss Christie.

Lizzie's job consisted of typing the letters which flowed in a ceaseless stream from Miss Dangerfield's pen, all more or less the same, all slightly different, so that her concentration often lapsed at the crucial moment, where a word or sentence was different. The bottom drawer where she hid all the paper she had messed up was full within a few weeks. Even filing made a welcome change, and going on an errand to another department was almost exciting.

Sandra and Sue did lots of typing as well, but they had a bit more variety, because they also dealt with telephone enquiries, which Lizzie didn't know enough about the work to help with. They also relieved their boredom with little chats scattered throughout the day. Lizzie sometimes joined in on these, sometimes she didn't bother. Often enough they were about Sue's boyfriends and Sandra's fiancé, and Lizzie found it hard to work up any enthsiasm about these topics. She got the feeling that Sue and Sandra sensed this and subtly resented it.

The great event of the day was the coffee break. At least it was a change of room. Usually it was nearly as boring as working, though. One day there was actually a serious discussion about the queen.

Miss Christie got quite carried away. 'When the Queen came here,' she was saying, 'which was about five years ago, we had a Reception for her, of course, and when she came into the room, it was quite extraordinary, she had this unmistakable *aura* about her. It was almost tangible. I'll never forget it. I had expected to be impressed, naturally, but — I found I simply couldn't take my eyes off her.' Her emotion was perfectly genuine.

It crossed Lizzie's mind that Miss Christie herself looked somewhat like the queen as she sat relating this story to her staff. After all, they were both upper-class women with a good deal of power and a gracious way of condescending to their subordinates.

The queen came up as a topic of conversation because Miss Dangerfield had looked up from her *Daily Telegraph* to mention that she was going to see the Royal Tournament that evening.

'I haven't been for a good many years,' she said, 'but I think we'll enjoy it.'

Gloria was most enthusiastic. 'Oh yes!' she exclaimed, 'my father always used to take us when we were little. It's splendid, isn't it. I like the horses best!'

'They do some marvellous stunts with motor cycles too, don't they,' put in Marcia. 'I saw some of it on the television.'

Lizzie dragged herself back to the typewriter.

When Miss Dangerfield left the office that evening she was tense. Most of the afternoon had been spent in fruitless phone calls, and a colleague from another department had popped in to see her right at the last moment, with an urgent problem which forced her to stay an extra fifteen minutes or so, just when she had hoped to get away quickly.

It had been cloudy all afternoon, and it started to drizzle just as she got into her car, which was most annoying because it would slow the traffic right down. The headlights and the traffic lights and the street lights, smeary in the wet, combined to give Miss Dangerfield the beginnings of a headache. There seemed to be all sorts of cyclists skidding around, dodging in and out of the cars, making her feel quite uneasy. Yesterday she had actually seen a man stick his arm out of his car window to signal, and knock a young woman right off her bike! Luckily she wasn't seriously hurt. On a day like this, when she was feeling a bit below par, Miss Dangerfield drove around in dread of causing an accident. She never had.

Finding somewhere to park was difficult as usual, and she got soaked on the way from the car to the restaurant. Once inside, she breathed a short sigh of relief. It was warm and cosy, if rather steamy. Condensation was running down the window panes. Miss Dangerfield cast her eyes round the room — Lilian had not yet arrived, it seemed. She took a seat at a corner table, snagging her tights as she did so, to her great irritation. A minute or two later she looked up from the menu to see Lilian standing just inside the door. Her mac was bundled round her in a most unstylish way. Her glasses had steamed up and she had to take them off, wipe them (on a grubby-looking handkerchief which she fished out of her capacious handbag) and replace them, before she could look round the room to pick out Miss Danger-field. As she caught sight of her, her face lit up with a beaming smile. She crossed the room to her friend's table with her idiosyncratic slow, low, almost bent-legged stride. She was getting even broader in the beam these days.

'Hello dear!' she cried warmly. 'What a shocker!' She plumped herself down in the opposite chair.

'Hello Lilian,' her friend replied, without much of a smile.

'What's the matter?' said Lilian, poking her head forward anxiously.

'Nothing. It's just that — I wish you wouldn't wear that scarf.' Lilian's face fell, and Miss Dangerfield could have bitten her tongue off. But she hated it when Lilian wore a scarf tied under her chin like that. It made her jaw look so square.

'Well, I suppose you would have preferred me to get soaking wet! I couldn't find my umbrella anywhere. Anyway, I suppose I can take it off now,' she conceded, her mild indignation evaporating immediately.

The two women had quite a cosy little meal together, and two glasses of wine helped to warm Miss Dangerfield up and calm her down. The frustrations of the day's work slid to rest in the silt at the bottom of her mind. She looked across at her friend, her companion of the past twenty-four years. Lilian had taken off her glasses again and was wiping them with a corner of the tablecloth. Her eyes still astonished Miss Dangerfield with their beauty. They were large and heavy-lidded. It was wretched that they had to be hidden behind her glasses all the time.

'Did you manage to get through to the decorators?' said Miss Dangerfield.

'Yes. They said they would be round on Saturday morning.'

Miss Dangerfield's irritation flared up again. 'But Lilian, I'm going to see Mother this weekend! I *told* you it would have to be a weekday, and I'd take some time off work!'

Miss Dangerfield had a tendency, which she tried fitfully to repress, to boss Lilian about. Lilian could give as good as she got though, when she thought it worth her while to lose her temper. This evening she didn't want to spoil things with a quarrel; they were supposed to be enjoying themselves. Luckily at this point their desserts were served, which gave them the opportunity to drop the contentious subject.

'How was school today?' asked Miss Dangerfield. Lilian was a classics teacher.

'Quite fun. We were discussing what hymns to have at the school anniversary service. Marian — Marian Marsh that is, the new music teacher, I've told you about her, she's quite young — she wants to have lots of modern ones, but I don't think you can beat the good old traditional tunes, do you?'

Miss Dangerfield agreed. She glanced at her watch and said she thought it was time for them to be on their way.

They both enjoyed the performance tremendously. The colour and the pageantry and above all the good humour of this display by Her Majesty's Armed Forces was most reassuring in a world where hijacks and terrorism seem to be the order of the day. How comforting to know that they had these dashing young men and their ingenious machinery on their side.

'Lilian,' said Miss Dangerfield when they were both tucked up in bed that night. 'Sorry I was grumpy earlier on this evening.'

Lilian turned to face her. 'Never mind darling, I didn't take it to heart.' Lilian shifted up slightly in the bed and placed a kiss on Miss Dangerfield's soft cheek. 'I could see you were tired.'

Miss Dangerfield put her arms around her neck and returned the kiss. Lilian was very sleepy, and soon turned on to her side, facing away from Miss Dangerfield, keeping hold of her arm around her waist. Both women curled up, so that Lilian was as it were sitting on Miss Dangerfield's lap. This was their favourite way for going to sleep.

Miss Dangerfield was tired by not sleepy. She was filled with overwhelming love and tenderness towards Lilian. They had been lovers for twenty-four years, nearly a quarter of a century, half of their lifetime, and still Miss Dangerfield found a thrill in her company and in her physical presence. She snuggled closer in, held her tighter. Lilian was asleep already. She could feel Lilian's soft round body next to her own. Well, they had grown middle-aged and fat together. They regarded themselves as married, united by a bond more durable than any wedding ceremony. The idea of parting was inconceivable, hurtful.

They had never really talked much about their relationship. Miss Dangerfield sometimes wondered what God thought about it. She hoped He didn't mind too much. She didn't like to dwell on that thought. Sometimes she liked to congratulate herself on the fact that she had had 'sex before marriage', as they used to call it, without ever risking a pregnancy, and somehow that seemed to indicate to her that God did look favourably on their union.

She and Lilian also prided themselves on the fact that in all this time, no one had ever guessed their secret. Not to their knowledge, at any rate. For appearances' sake, each had a bedroom of her own, but only if they had guests did they actually sleep separately: usually they slept in Lilian's room. They were regarded as two spinsters who had somehow missed the boat to marriage, and lived together for company. It gave Miss Dangerfield quite a kick to think how she and Lilian, who in everything else were such conservative souls, had succeeded in deceiving the whole world! Even her brother — and he was a barrister, who spent a lot of his time prosecuting people for all sorts of irregularities — had no idea of an 'irregularity' taking place within his own family circle.

And having come to this comforting conclusion for the hundredth time, Miss Dangerfield finally fell asleep.

The last week that Lizzie worked in the department, one of the typists was on holiday, and a temp called Sally came to take her place. She talked incessantly. The others were treated to a running commentary on her every typing error, as well as full details of her outside life, her boyfriend, her mother, her room-mate, her room-mate's new cardigan, etc. Lizzie hated her.

One coffee break Miss Dangerfield came in to find the younger women all having to listen to Sally describe how in the hostel she had recently lived in, they were not allowed to watch television after 11 o'clock.

'Not even if there's a good film on that's halfway through,' Sally was saying. 'Like I wanted to watch *The Killing of Sister George* when that was on, but we weren't allowed to. It was really annoying.'

'I saw that,' said Sandra. 'It was really creepy. Do you know, the club in the last scene of that film is a *real lesbian club*. It's really revolting, isn't it?'

The colour rose to Lizzie's cheeks. 'I suppose you think all lesbians are murderers and perverts and sado-masochists or something,' she said in a loud grating voice, 'living in a twilight world.' All eyes were turned towards her, except those of Miss Dangerfield. 'Well, I happen to be a lesbian, so that just proves you wrong, doesn't it. Because I'm a typist, the same as you.' Sally looked at her blankly. Sandra opened her eyes wide, and turned to Sally to change the subject.

'How do you like your new flat?'

'I think it's going to be fine,' said Sally. 'We've still got loads of work to do on it though.'

'Have you met any of the neighbours?' Sandra inquired, anxious to keep the conversation going.

'Oh, we're surrounded by queers!' Sally giggled. 'There's two upstairs, and one on the ground floor, and more next door. They all mince around like anything.'

There was a pause.

'Oh well,' said Sandra recklessly, 'at least you'll be safe.'

Lizzie was white with anger and distress. She had come to work that morning bleary-eyed but happy after a night of love with a woman called Paula. Well, not so much a night of love as a night of high jinks, a night of delight. The infinite softness of Paula's body and the sharpness of her wit had combined to give Lizzie a tender thrill. They hardly knew each other, they might not meet again for ages, but Lizzie felt that for once they had stumbled on that rare treasure, sex without pain, without possessiveness, without plans for the future, sex without exploitation and humiliation; the jewel in the lotus. So she had only had three hours' sleep, but she had come to work in hazy high spirits, only to bang her head against the wall of other people's fears.

Gloria and Sandra and Marcia were exchanging looks which were a mixture of surprise, embarrassment and amusement.

Miss Dangerfield hated scenes. She was only glad Miss Christie wasn't present. She decided to take her coffee back to her office, and left the room, involuntarily singing softly to herself, in her characteristic way.

Lizzie swore at Sally and walked out, slamming the door behind her.

A murmur of embarrassed laughter rippled around those remaining in the room.

'Well!' exclaimed Marcia. 'Who would have thought it? I'm absolutely amazed!'

'Now we know why she keeps her hair so short,' said Gloria solemnly, 'and always wears trousers.'

Sally said nothing at all.

Back in her office, Miss Dangerfield immersed herself in a tough administrative problem. But she found it hard to concentrate for the rest of the day.

She kept wondering if what she had just seen and heard had actually taken place. There were two huge reasons for her to be surprised. The first was, to think that this young girl Lizzie, whom she had always assumed would have a boyfriend and so on, just like all the others, who was so ordinary really, and quite a good worker, but whom she hadn't paid much attention to, was — was like her. And the second extraordinary thing, well, she didn't know which of the two was the most extraordinary really, was that she admitted it. She actually said, 'I'm a lesbian.' She actually used that word.

Now, Miss Dangerfield of course had heard of 'Gay Lib', if only in the pages of the *Daily Telegraph*, but quite honestly she had not paid it very much attention. For one thing, she had vaguely imagined it only referred to men. For another thing, it always struck her as being incredibly undignified and vulgar. There was no need to go around drawing attention to yourself like that. Why should the rest of the world want to know? Leave them alone and they'll leave you alone, that's what she had always found. Just imagine, if everyone knew about her and Lilian! Life would be intolerable! Lilian would lose her job for sure. And just imagine, if her mother and brother found out! Her mother was seventy-nine! The shock would kill her. No, it simply wasn't fair to burden everyone else with the truth like that. The thought of how it would affect her mother was conclusive proof, as it were, of the impossibility of Miss Dangerfield ever telling the world the truth about herself.

Lizzie didn't recover for the rest of the day either. She was glad she had come out to her fellow workers at long last, but angry with herself to have mishandled it so badly. If she wasn't such a coward she would have come out right at the beginning and this crisis would have been avoided. Anyone could come out during their last week in a job, big deal, she wouldn't have to meet any of these people ever again. She wasn't sorry she had lost her temper, they all needed shaking up, they were so safe and complacent. But she was sorry that she wasn't going to be there long enough now to talk to any of them properly. She would leave them as confused and prejudiced as she had found them. She was overwhelmed with tiredness and depression.

That day seemed endless, but when it finally did grind to a halt, she slouched off and spent the evening getting drunk with someone she didn't like very much, then spent the night in a lagery stupor, going over and over the events of the day in an interminable repetitive dream.

Miss Dangerfield's sleep that night was similarly unrefreshing, and when she got to work the next morning she walked into the general office only to come face to face with a frightful badge Lizzie was wearing. It said 'Lesbians Ignite'. All at once she remembered an appalling dream she had had last night in which she had been making love with Lilian — no, it was with Lizzie! — when suddenly her mother had walked in and caught them. She gave a nervous laugh and darted round Lizzie to get at the filing cabinet.

At that moment, Miss Christie entered the room, accompanied by the head of one of the other departments, a pompous fellow called Walter Phillips. Miss Christie caught sight of the offending badge, coloured, faltered for a moment, then stiffened. She completed her business with Mr Phillips, watched him go, and then summoned Lizzie into her office. Miss Dangerfield waited a second or two before following them out.

In the corridor she caught a glimpse of Lizzie just disappearing into Miss Christie's room. She went into her own office. The interconnecting door was shut, but as usual she could hear fairly clearly all that passed in the other office.

'Elizabeth,' Miss Christie was saying, 'I'm sure you know why I've called you in.'

There was no reply. Miss Dangerfield could picture Lizzie scowling and biting her lip. As a matter of fact she was wrong — Lizzie's face was a complete blank, which in a way Miss Christie found even more exasperating, as it forced her to make all the effort herself.

'I must ask you to remove that badge,' she said at last.

'Well really, Miss Christie,' said Lizzie, sounding sullen, 'I don't see why I should. If it's all the same to you,' she added foolishly.

'It's *not* all the same to me,' said Miss Christie gravely, 'as I'm sure you will appreciate. What you mean by wearing such a badge, I dread to think. Really, you've gone too far. You must see that.'

Lizzie remained stubbornly silent, and Miss Dangerfield, listening intently in the adjoining room, did not envy Miss Christie her task at all, though she could see it had to be done.

'You've been such a help to us, Lizzie,' — Miss Christie was obviously trying a different approach — 'and you've done your work so quickly and so efficiently' — her voice hesitated for a moment; perhaps she had caught Lizzie's green eye at that point — 'and we're going to miss you very much when you leave us at the end of the week; it just seems a great pity if you have to spoil things at this stage.'

'But Miss Christie,' protested Lizzie, 'that's just the point. I'm here to do a job, my work's been all right, you say so yourself — so what's my sex life got to do with it?'

Miss Dangerfield winced.

'Elizabeth,' said Miss Christie, and now her voice was both stern and complacent, for she felt that what she was saying was irrefutable. 'Elizabeth, what you do in your own private life is your own concern. It is not my place to make any comment upon it, and quite frankly, in the circumstances I would rather not know about it.' She gave the last few words their due emphasis.

'As I say, it's none of my business. *I do not want to know.* And I think it is very unfair of you to impose your own ideas on this subject on everyone else.' Her voice became slightly tremulous towards the end of this pronouncement.

'Well, everyone else imposes their heterosexuality on me.' This reply meant nothing to either Miss Christie or Miss Dangerfield. Lizzie tried to explain what she was getting at.

'Take Sandra's wedding, for instance. We've had talk of nothing else all week — "Is it going to be a white wedding?" "Where are they going for their honeymoon?" "Aren't they lucky to have a house lined up ready for them!" '

'In other words,' interrupted Miss Christie, 'you're jealous.'

'Jealous!' repeated Lizzie, her voice squeaky with indignation. She had met the bridegroom-to-be, and he was horrible. He teased Sandra almost incessantly.

'I wouldn't change my life with theirs for a million pounds,' persisted Lizzie. 'I don't want a diamond engagement ring. I don't want a husband to look after me. I can look after myself. Like you've done, Miss Christie.' The elderly woman said nothing. 'And I'm just sick and tired of hearing about their boyfriends and their husbands and their in-laws. If I *am* jealous, all I'm jealous of is the chance to talk about my life openly like everyone else does, without being regarded as a freak. I love other women, I'm not ashamed of what I am and I won't keep quiet about it any longer. Why should I?'

Miss Dangerfield's heart was palpitating. How would Miss Christie answer that?

'You are very young, Lizzie,' said Miss Christie with calm deliberation, 'but until today you always impressed me as being quite mature for your age, and I am surprised to find that you do not seem to understand the way society works. In a community we have to think of other people. Whether you like it or not, you and your kind are a minority, and your — practices are simply not acceptable to the vast majority of people. We all have to make some compromises, you know, if we are to get along with each other tolerably well.' Miss Christie paused, well aware of how inadequate what she was saying was as an expression of all she so passionately believed in. Lizzie at least was grateful that she had not attempted to suggest that the real problem was that she 'had not yet met the right man'.

'We're not such a small minority as you think. I bet you are acquainted with other lesbians besides me.'

Miss Christie shrank from the terrible word. Behind the door, Miss Dangerfield blushed.

'But how could that be, Elizabeth? How could I be acquainted with these — women — and not be aware of the fact?'

'*Because*,' said Lizzie, almost between clenched teeth, 'they are afraid to say so . . .'

'If they are afraid to say so then they must be ashamed of what they are,' interposed Miss Christie.

'No, no,' Lizzie insisted, 'it's because they are afraid of how other people will react, that's all. Like you — I wear a lesbian badge and you tell me to take it off. You're my boss, it's hard for me to disobey. I happen to be leaving at the end of the week but if I wasn't you could sack me. I wear a lesbian badge and the others all snigger at me behind my back. So what would be the easiest thing? To take the badge off, of course. But then you wouldn't know I was a lesbian, would you? How do you know you've never seen any lesbians? If they're not wearing badges they look just like ordinary people. Which we are.'

Lizzie felt silent. She hadn't wanted to upset Miss Christie, but there didn't seem any way to avoid it.

The older woman felt as if she had been assaulted. Something was stirring inside her but for the time being she could not afford to examine it too closely.

'We seem to have strayed somewhat from the point,' she said at length. 'I don't think we're ever going to see eye to eye about this, so all I can say is, *for my sake*, please remove the badge.' Lizzie appeared to be softening. The image of Mr Phillips rose up in Miss Christie's mind. 'We have the reputation of the department to think of, after all.' Lizzie bristled once again, and Miss Christie realised she had made a tactical error. Lizzie was susceptible to a personal appeal, but for some reason seemed impervious to an appeal on the grounds of the good of the community in which she worked. 'It's only for three more days after all. I know you won't let me down, my dear.'

'Miss Christie,' said Lizzie, 'there is one more thing I would like to mention. Yesterday at coffee time the others were making all sorts of remarks about "queers" and so on, which I found extremely offensive, and that's really the main reason why I wore this badge today.'

Miss Christie turned her head sympathetically on one side. 'Well, I'm sorry they hurt your feelings, but I'm sure they never meant to be unkind. After all, they were not to know that you would take it personally.'

The two women were at deadlock. Lizzie was tempted to take off the badge to spare Miss Christie further pain. But she felt great resistance to the notion of capitulating to pressure from an employer in this way. How much easier it would have been if her boss had been a man. She could have attributed his intractability to hurt vanity, and she would have enjoyed provoking him. But the fact that Miss Christie was a woman made it much harder for Lizzie to hold out against her entreaties.

Miss Christie, on the other hand, had been more moved and convinced by Lizzie's words than she would admit even to herself. She certainly identified with her staunch determination to remain independent of men. She herself would never have risen to the position she had attained if she had got married and had a family. But her passionate conservatism, her dread of novelty and her love for all that was traditional and right and proper, her respect for the values that had been tested and approved by the community as a whole over countless centuries, all these were violated by this child's outrageous claims.

Behind the door Miss Dangerfield listened to the silence. Her whole being was in a turmoil. She could stand it no longer, and abruptly escaped into the corridor. She went to the toilet to sit down and think quietly for a minute, but the more she tried to think the more confused she got. All sorts of things were screaming at her until she thought her head would burst. It would be impossible for her to do any more work that day, she must get home and go to bed, to sleep, to oblivion.

She hung about in the toilet as long as she could to make sure that by the time she got back to her office the interview in the adjoining room would be over. She was lucky — it was. She steeled herself to go in to see Miss Christie and tell her she wasn't feeling well.

'Yes, you do look very flushed, Irene, by all means go home and lie down,' said Miss Christie. 'This is very sudden, isn't it?'

This story has been cut slightly from the original which can be read in Everyday Matters: New Short Stories by Women, Vol. 1, Sheba Feminist Publishers.

PAUL THEROUX

White Lies

Normally, in describing the life cycle of ectoparasites for my notebook, I went into great detail, since I hoped to publish an article about the strangest ones when I returned home from Africa. The one exception was *Dermatobia bendiense*. I could not give it my name; I was not its victim. And the description? One word: *Jerry*. I needed nothing more to remind me of the discovery, and though I fully intend to test my findings in the pages of an entomological journal, the memory is still too horrifying for me to reduce it to science.

Jerry Benda and I shared a house on the compound of a bush school. Every Friday and Saturday night he met an African girl named Ameena at the Rainbow Bar and brought her home in a taxi. There was no scandal: no one knew. In the morning, after breakfast, Ameena did Jerry's ironing (I did my own) and the black cook carried her back to town on the crossbar of his old bike. That was a hilarious sight. Returning from my own particular passion, which was collecting insects in the fields near our house, I often met them on the road: Jika in his cook's khakis and skullcap pedaling the long-legged Ameena — I must say, she reminded me of a highly desirable insect. They yelped as they clattered down the road, the deep ruts making the bicycle bell hiccup like an alarm clock. A stranger would have assumed these Africans were man and wife, making an early morning foray to the market. The local people paid no attention.

Only I knew that these were the cook and mistress of a young American who was regarded at the school as very charming in his manner and serious in his work. The cook's laughter was a nervous giggle — he was afraid of Ameena. But he was devoted to Jerry and far too loyal to refuse to do what Jerry asked of him.

Jerry was deceitful, but at the time I did not think he was imaginative enough to do any damage. And yet his was not the conventional double life that most white people led in Africa. Jerry had certain ambitions: ambition makes more liars than egotism does. But Jerry was so careful, his lies such modest calculations, he was always believed. He said he was from Boston. 'Belmont actually,' he told me, when I said I was from Medford. His passport — *Bearer's address* — said Watertown. He felt he had to conceal it. That explained a lot: the insecurity of living on the lower slopes of the long hill, between the smoldering steeples of Boston and the clean, high-priced air of Belmont. We are probably no more class conscious than the British, but when we make class an issue it seems more than snobbery. It becomes a bizarre spectacle, a kind of attention seeking, and I cannot hear an American speaking of his social position without thinking of a human fly, one of those tiny men in grubby capes whom one sometimes sees clinging to the brickwork of a tall building.

What had begun as fantasy had, after six months of his repeating it in our insignificant place, made it seem like fact. Jerry didn't know Africa: his one girl friend stood for the whole continent. And of course he lied to her. I had the impression that it was one of the reasons Jerry wanted to stay in Africa. If you tell enough lies about yourself, they take hold. It becomes impossible ever to go back, since that means facing the truth. In Africa, no one could dispute what Jerry said he was: a wealthy Bostonian, from a family of some distinction, adventuring in Third World philanthropy before inheriting his father's business.

Re-reading the above, I think I may be misrepresenting him. Although he was undeniably a fraud in some ways, his fraudulence was the last thing you noticed about him. What you saw first was a tall good-natured person in his early twenties, confidently casual, with easy charm and a gift for ingenious flattery. When I told him I had majored in entomology he called me 'Doctor.' This later became 'Doc.' He showed exaggerated respect to the gardeners and washerwomen at the school, using the politest phrases when he spoke to them. He always said 'sir' to the students ('You, sir, are a lazy little creep'), which baffled them and won them over. The cook adored him, and even the cook's cook — who was lame and fourteen and ragged — liked Jerry to the point where the poor boy would go through the compound stealing flowers from the Inkpens' garden to decorate our table. While I was merely tolerated as an unattractive and near-sighted bug collector, Jerry was courted by the British wives in the compound. The wife of the new headmaster, Lady Alice (Sir Godfrey Inkpen had been knighted for his work in the Civil Service) usually stopped in to see Jerry when her husband was away. Jerry was gracious with her and anxious to make a good impression. Privately, he said, 'She's all tits and teeth.'

'Why is it,' he said to me one day, 'that the white women have all the money and the black ones have all the looks?'

'I didn't realize you were interested in money.'

'Not for itself, Doc,' he said. 'I'm interested in what it can buy.'

No matter how hard I tried, I could not get used to hearing Ameena's squawks of pleasure from the next room, or Jerry's elbows banging against the wall. At any moment, I expected their humpings and slappings to bring down the boxes of mounted butterflies I had hung there. At breakfast, Jerry was his urbane self, sitting at the head of the table while Ameena cackled.

He held a teapot in each hand. 'What will it be, my dear? Chinese or Indian tea? Marmalade or jam? Poached or scrambled? And may I suggest a kipper?

'*Wopusa!*' Ameena would say. 'Idiot!'

She was lean, angular, and wore a scarf in a handsome turban on her head. 'I'd marry that girl tomorrow,' Jerry said, 'if she had fifty grand.' Her breasts were full and her skin was like velvet; she looked majestic, even doing the ironing. And when I saw her ironing, it struck me how Jerry inspired devotion in people.

But not any from me. I think I resented him because he was new. I had been in Africa for two years and had replaced any ideas of sexual conquest with the possibility of a great entomological discovery. But he was not interested in my experience. There was a great deal I could have told him. In the meantime, I watched Jika taking Ameena into town on his bicycle, and I added specimens to my collection.

Then, one day, the Inkpens' daughter arrived from Rhodesia to spend her school holidays with her parents.

We had seen her the day after she arrived, admiring the roses in her mother's garden, which adjoined ours. She was about seventeen, and breathless and damp; and so small I at once imagined this pink butterfly struggling in my net. Her name was Petra (her parents called her 'Pet'), and her pretty bloom was recklessness and innocence. Jerry said, 'I'm going to marry her.'

'I've been thinking about it,' he said the next day. 'If I just invite her I'll look like a wolf. If I invite the three of them it'll seem as if I'm stage-managing it. So I'll invite the parents — for some inconvenient time — and they'll have no choice but to ask me if they can bring the daughter along, too. *They'll* ask *me* if they can bring her. Good thinking? It'll have to be after dark — they'll be afraid of someone raping her. Sunday's always family day, so how about Sunday at seven? High tea. They will deliver her into my hands.'

The invitation was accepted. And Sir Godfrey said, 'I hope you don't mind if we bring our daughter . . .'

More than anything, I wished to see whether Jerry would bring Ameena home that Saturday night. He did — I suppose he did not want to arouse Ameena's suspicions — and on Sunday morning it was breakfast as usual and 'What will it be, my dear?'

But everything was not as usual. In the kitchen, Jika was making a cake and scones. The powerful fragrance of baking, so early on a Sunday morning, made Ameena curious. She sniffed and smiled and picked up her cup. Then she asked: What was the cook making?

'Cakes,' said Jerry. He smiled back at her.

Jika entered timidly with some toast.

'You're a better cook than I am,' Ameena said in Chinyanja. 'I don't know how to make cakes.'

Jika looked terribly worried. He glanced at Jerry.

'Have a cake,' said Jerry to Ameena.

Ameena tipped the cup to her lips and said slyly, 'Africans don't eat cakes for breakfast.'

'*We* do,' said Jerry, with guilty rapidity. 'It's an old American custom.'

Ameena was staring at Jika. When she stood up he winced.

Ameena said, 'I have to make water.' It was one of the few English sentences she knew.

Jerry said, 'I think she suspects something.'

As I started to leave with my net and my chloroform bottle I heard a great fuss in the kitchen, Jerry telling Ameena not to do the ironing, Ameena protesting, Jika groaning. But Jerry was angry, and soon the bicycle was bumping away from the house: Jika pedaling, Ameena on the crossbar.

'She just wanted to hang around,' said Jerry. 'Guess what the bitch was doing? She was ironing a drip-dry shirt!'

It was early evening when the Inkpens arrived, but night fell before tea was poured. Petra sat between her proud parents, saying what a super house we had, what a super school it was, how super it was to have a holiday here. Her monotonous ignorance made her even more desirable.

Perhaps for our benefit — to show her off — Sir Godfrey asked her leading questions. 'Mother tells me you've taken up knitting' and 'Mother says you've become quite a whiz at maths.' Now he said, 'I hear you've been doing some riding.'

'Heaps, actually,' said Petra. Her face was shining. 'There are some stables near the school.'

Dances, exams, picnics, house parties: Petra gushed about her Rhodesian school. And in doing so she made it seem a distant place — not an African country at all, but a special preserve of superior English recreations.

'That's funny,' I said. 'Aren't there Africans there?'

Jerry looked sharply at me.

'Not at the school,' said Petra. 'There are some in town. The girls call them nig-nogs.' She smiled. 'But they're quite sweet actually.'

'The Africans, dear?' asked Lady Alice.

'The girls,' said Petra.

Her father frowned.

Jerry said, 'What do you think of this place?'

'Honestly, I think it's super.'

'Too bad it's so dark at the moment,' said Jerry. 'I'd like to show you my frangipani.'

'Jerry's famous for that frangipani,' said Lady Alice.

Jerry had gone to the French windows to indicate the general direction of the bush. He gestured toward the darkness and said, 'It's somewhere over there.'

'I see it,' said Petra.

The white flowers and the twisted limbs of the frangipani were clearly visible in the headlights of an approaching car.

Sir Godfrey said, 'I think you have a visitor.'

The Inkpens were staring at the taxi. I watched Jerry. He had turned pale, but kept his composure. 'Ah, yes,' he said, 'it's the sister of one of our pupils.' He stepped outside to intercept her, but Ameena was too quick for him. She hurried past him, into the parlor where the Inkpens sat dumbfounded. Then Sir Godfrey, who had been surprised into silence, stood up and offered Ameena his chair.

Ameena gave a nervous grunt and faced Jerry. She wore the black satin cloak and sandals of a village Muslim. I had never seen her in anything but a tight dress and high heels; in that long cloak she looked like a very dangerous fly which had buzzed into the room on stiff wings.

'How nice to see you,' said Jerry. Every word was right, but his voice had become shrill. 'I'd like you to meet . . .'

Ameena flapped the wings of her cloak in embarrassment and said, 'I cannot stay. And I am sorry for this visit.' She spoke in her own language. Her voice was calm and even apologetic.

'Perhaps she'd like to sit down,' said Sir Godfrey, who was still standing.

'I think she's fine,' said Jerry, backing away slightly.

Now I saw the look of horror on Petra's face. She glanced up and down, from the dark shawled head to the cracked feet, then gaped in bewilderment and fear.

At the kitchen door, Jika stood with his hands over his ears.

'Let's go outside,' said Jerry in Chinyanja.

'It is not necessary,' said Ameena. 'I have something for you. I can give it to you here.'

Jika ducked into the kitchen and shut the door.

'Here,' said Ameena. She fumbled with her cloak.

Jerry said quickly, 'No,' and turned as if to avert the thrust of a dagger.

But Ameena had taken a soft gift-wrapped parcel from the folds of her cloak. She handed it to Jerry and, without turning to us, flapped out of the room. She became invisible as soon as she stepped into the darkness. Before anyone could speak, the taxi was speeding away from the house.

Lady Alice said, 'How very odd.'

'Just a courtesy call,' said Jerry, and amazed me with a succession of plausible lies. 'Her brother's in Form Four — a very bright boy, as a matter of fact. She was rather pleased by how well he'd done in his exams. She stopped in to say thanks.'

'That's *very* African,' said Sir Godfrey.

'It's lovely when people drop in,' said Petra. 'It's really quite a compliment.'

Jerry was smiling weakly and eyeing the window, as if he expected Ameena to thunder in once again and split his head open. Or perhaps not. Perhaps he was congratulating himself that it had all gone so smoothly.

Lady Alice said, 'Well, aren't you going to open it?'

'Open what?' said Jerry, and then he realized that he was holding the parcel. 'You mean this?'

'I wonder what it could be,' said Petra.

I prayed that it was nothing frightening. I had heard stories of jilted lovers sending aborted fetuses to the men who had wronged them.

'I adore opening parcels,' said Petra.

Jerry tore off the wrapping paper, but satisfied himself that it was nothing incriminating before he showed it to the Inkpens.

'Is it a shirt?' said Lady Alice.

'It's a beauty,' said Sir Godfrey.

It was red and yellow and green, with embroidery at the collar and cuffs; an African design. Jerry said, 'I should give it back. It's a sort of bribe, isn't it?'

'Absolutely not,' said Sir Godfrey. 'I insist you keep it.'

'Put it on!' said Petra.

Jerry shook his head. Lady Alice said, 'Oh, do!'

'Some other time,' said Jerry. He tossed the shirt aside and told a long humorous story of his sister's wedding reception on the family yacht. And before the Inkpens left he asked Sir Godfrey with old-fashioned formality if he might be allowed to take Petra on a day trip to the local tea estate.

'You're welcome to use my car if you like,' said Sir Godfrey.

It was only after the Inkpens had gone that Jerry began to

tremble. He tottered to a chair, lit a cigarette, and said, 'That was the worst hour of my life. Did you see her? Jesus! I thought that was the end. But what did I tell you? She suspected something!'

'Not necessarily,' I said.

He kicked the shirt — I noticed he was hesitant to touch it — and said, 'What's this all about then?'

'As you told Inky — it's a present.'

'She's a witch,' said Jerry. 'She's up to something.'

'You're crazy,' I said. 'What's more, you're unfair. You kicked her out of the house. She came back to ingratiate herself by giving you a present — a new shirt for all the ones she didn't have a chance to iron. But she saw our neighbors. I don't think she'll be back.'

'What amazes me,' said Jerry, 'is your presumption. I've been sleeping with Ameena for six months, while you've been playing with yourself. And here you are trying to tell me about her! You're incredible.'

Jerry had the worst weakness of the liar: he never believed anything you told him.

I said, 'What are you going to do with the shirt?'

Clearly this had been worrying him. But he said nothing.

Late that night, working with my specimens, I smelled acrid smoke. I went to the window. The incinerator was alight; Jika was coughing and stirring the flames with a stick.

The next Saturday, Jerry took Petra to the tea estate in Sir Godfrey's gray Humber. I spent the day with my net, rather resenting the thought that Jerry had all the luck. First Ameena, now Petra. And he had ditched Ameena. There seemed no end to his arrogance or — what was more annoying — his luck. He came back to the house alone. I vowed that I would not give him a chance to do any sexual boasting. I stayed in my room, but less than ten minutes after he arrived home he was knocking on my door.

'I'm busy,' I yelled.

'Doc, this is serious.'

He entered rather breathless, fever-white and apologetic. This was not someone who had just made a sexual conquest — I knew as soon as I saw him that it had all gone wrong. So I said, 'How does she bump?'

He shook his head. He looked very pale. He said, 'I couldn't.'

'So she turned you down.' I could not hide my satisfaction.

'She was screaming for it,' he said, rather primly. 'She's seventeen, Doc. She's locked in a girls' school half the year. She even found a convenient haystack. But I had to say no. In fact, I couldn't get away from her fast enough.'

'Something *is* wrong,' I said. 'Do you feel all right?'

He ignored the question. 'Doc,' he said, 'remember when Ameena barged in. Just think hard. Did she touch me? Listen, this is important.'

I told him I could not honestly remember whether she had touched him. The incident was so pathetic and embarrassing I had tried to blot it out.

'I knew something like this was going to happen. But I don't understand it.' He was talking quickly and unbuttoning his shirt. Then he took it off. 'Look at this. Have you ever seen anything like it?'

At first I thought his body was covered by welts. But what I had taken to be welts were a mass of tiny reddened patches, like fly bites, some already swollen into bumps. Most of them — and by far the worst — were on his back and shoulders. They were as ugly as acne and had given his skin that same shine of infection.

'It's interesting,' I said.

'Interesting!' he screamed. 'It looks like syphilis and all you can say is it's interesting. Thanks a lot.'

'Does it hurt?'

'Not too much,' he said. 'I noticed it this morning before I went out. But I think they've gotten worse. That's why nothing happened with Petra. I was too scared to take my shirt off.'

'I'm sure she wouldn't have minded if you'd kept it on.'

'I couldn't risk it,' he said. 'What if it's contagious?'

He put calamine lotion on it and covered it carefully with gauze, and the next day it was worse. Each small bite had swelled to a pimple, and some of them seemed on the point of erupting: a mass of small warty boils. That was on Sunday. On Monday I told Sir Godfrey that Jerry had a bad cold and could not teach. When I got back to the house that afternoon, Jerry said that it was so painful he couldn't lie down. He had spent the afternoon sitting bolt upright in a chair.

'It was that shirt,' he said. 'Ameena's shirt. She did something to it.'

I said, 'You're lying. Jika burned that shirt — remember?'

'She touched me,' he said. 'Doc, maybe it's not a curse — I'm not superstitious anyway. Maybe she gave me syph.'

'Let's hope so.'

'What do you mean by that!'

'I mean, there's a cure for syphilis.'

'Suppose it's not that?'

'We're in Africa,' I said.

This terrified him, as I knew it would.

He said, 'Look at my back and tell me if it looks as bad as it feels.'

He crouched under the lamp. His back was grotesquely inflamed. The eruptions had become like nipples, much bigger and with a bruised discoloration. I pressed one. He cried out. Watery liquid leaked from a pustule.

'That hurt!' he said.

'Wait.' I saw more infection inside the burst boil — a white clotted mass. I told him to grit his teeth. 'I'm going to squeeze this one.'

I pressed it between my thumbs and as I did a small white knob protruded. It was not pus — not liquid. I kept on pressing and Jerry yelled with shrill ferocity until I was done. Then I showed him what I had squeezed from his back; it was on the tip of my tweezers — a live maggot.

'It's a worm!'

'A larva.'

'You know about these things. You've seen this before, haven't you?'

I told him the truth. I had never seen one like it before in my life. It was not in any textbook I had ever seen. And I told him more: there were, I said, perhaps two hundred of them, just like the one wriggling on my tweezers, in those boils on his body.

Jerry began to cry.

That night I heard him writhing in his bed, and groaning, and if I had not known him better I would have thought Ameena was with him. He turned and jerked and thumped like a lover maddened by desire; and he whimpered, too, seeming to savor the kind of pain that is indistinguishable from sexual pleasure. But it was no more passion than the movement of those maggots in his flesh. In the morning, gray with sleeplessness, he said he felt like a corpse. Truly, he looked as if he was being eaten alive.

An illness you read about is never as bad as the real thing. Boy Scouts are told to suck the poison out of snakebites. But a snakebite — swollen and black and running like a leper's sore — is so horrible I can't imagine anyone capable of staring at it, much less putting his mouth on it. It was that way with Jerry's boils. All the textbooks on earth could not have prepared me for their ugliness, and what made them even more repellent was the fact that his face and hands were free of them. He was infected from his neck to his waist, and down his arms; his face was haggard, and in marked contrast to his sores.

I said, 'We'll have to get you to a doctor.'

'A witch doctor.'

'You're serious!'

He gasped and said, 'I'm dying, Doc. You have to help me.'

'We can borrow Sir Godfrey's car. We could be in Blantyre by midnight.'

Jerry said, 'I can't last until midnight.'

'Take it easy,' I said. 'I have to go over to the school. I'll say you're still sick. I don't have any classes this afternoon, so when I get back I'll see if I can do anything for you.'

'There are witch doctors around here,' he said. 'You can find one — they know what to do. It's a curse.'

I watched his expression change as I said, 'Maybe it's the curse of the white worm.' He deserved to suffer, after what he had done, but his face was so twisted in fear, I added, 'There's only one thing to do. Get those maggots out. It might work.'

'Why did I come to this fucking place!'

But he shut his eyes and was silent: he knew why he had left home.

When I returned from the school ('And how is our ailing friend?' Sir Godfrey had asked at morning assembly), the house seemed empty. I had a moment of panic, thinking that Jerry — unable to stand the pain — had taken an overdose. I ran into the bedroom. He lay asleep on his side, but woke when I shock him.

'Where's Jika?' I said.

'I gave him the week off,' said Jerry. 'I didn't want him to see me. What are you doing?'

I had set out a spirit lamp and my surgical tools: tweezers, a scalpel, cotton, alcohol, bandages. He grew afraid when I shut the door and shone the lamp on him.

'I don't want you to do it,' he said. 'You don't know anything about this. You said you'd never seen this thing before.'

I said, 'Do you want to die?'

He sobbed and lay flat on the bed. I bent over him to begin. The maggots had grown larger, some had broken the skin, and their ugly heads stuck out like beads. I lanced the worst boil, between his shoulder blades. Jerry cried out and arched his back, but I kept digging and prodding, and I found that heat made it simpler. If I held my cigarette lighter near the wound the maggot wriggled, and by degrees, I eased it out. The danger lay in their breaking: if I pulled too hard some would be left in the boil to decay, and that I said would kill him.

By the end of the afternoon I had removed only twenty or so, and Jerry had fainted from the pain. He woke at nightfall. He looked at the saucer beside the bed and saw the maggots jerking in it — they had worked themselves into a white knot — and he screamed. I had to hold him until he calmed down. And then I continued.

I kept at it until very late. And I must admit that it gave me a certain pleasure. It was not only that Jerry deserved to suffer for his deceit — and his suffering was that of a condemned man; but also what I told him had been true: this was a startling discovery for me, as an entomologist. I had never seen such creatures before.

It was after midnight when I stopped. My hand ached, my eyes hurt from the glare, and I was sick to my stomach. Jerry had gone to sleep. I switched off the light and left him to his nightmares.

He was slightly better by morning. He was still pale, and the opened boils were crusted with blood, but he had more life in him than I had seen for days. And yet he was brutally scarred. I think he knew this: he looked as if he had been whipped.

'You saved my life,' he said.

'Give it a few days,' I said.

He smiled. I knew what he was thinking. Like all liars — those

people who behave like human flies on our towering credulity —
he was preparing his explanation. But this would be a final reply:
he was preparing his escape.

'I'm leaving,' he said. 'I've got some money — and there's a
night bus — ' He stopped speaking and looked at my desk.
'What's that?'

It was the dish of maggots, now as full as a rice pudding.

'Get rid of them!'

'I want to study them,' I said. 'I think I've earned the right to do
that. But I'm off to morning assembly — what shall I tell Inky?'

'Tell him I might have this cold for a long time.'

He was gone when I got back to the house; his room had been
emptied, and he'd left me his books and his tennis racket with a
note. I made what explanations I could. I told the truth: I had no
idea where he had gone. A week later, Petra went back to
Rhodesia, but she told me she would be back. As we chatted over
the fence I heard Jerry's voice: *She's screaming for it.* I said, 'We'll
go horseback riding.'

'Super!'

The curse of the white worm: Jerry had believed me. But it was
the curse of impatience — he had been impatient to get rid of
Ameena, impatient for Petra, impatient to put on a shirt that had
not been ironed. What a pity it was that he was not around when
the maggots hatched, to see them become flies I had never seen.
He might have admired the way I expertly pickled some and
sealed others in plastic and mounted twenty of them on a tray.

And what flies they were! It was a species that was not in any
book, and yet the surprising thing was that in spite of their
differently shaped wings (like a Muslim woman's cloak) and the
shape of their bodies (a slight pinch above the thorax, giving
them rather attractive waists), their life cycle was the same as
many others of their kind: they laid their eggs on laundry and
these larvae hatched at body heat and burrowed into the skin to
mature. Of course, laundry was always ironed — even drip-dry
shirts — to kill them. Everyone who knew Africa knew that.

ALEX LA GUMA

Coffee for the Road

They were past the maize-lands and driving through the wide, low, semi-desert country that sprawled away on all sides in reddish brown flats and depressions. The land, going south, was scattered with scrub and thorn bushes, like a vast unswept carpet. Far to the right, the metal vanes of a windmill pump turned wearily in the faint morning breeze, as if it had just been wakened to set reluctantly about its duty of sucking water from the miserly earth. The car hurtled along the asphalt road, its tyres roaring along the black surface.

'I want another sandwich, please,' Zaida said. She huddled in the blanketed space among the suitcases in the back. She was six years old and weary from the long, speeding journey, and her initial interest in the landscape had evaporated, so that now she sagged tiredly in the padded space, ignoring the parched gullies and stunted trees that whisked past.

'There's some in the tin. You can help yourself, can't you?' the woman at the wheel said, without taking her eyes off the road. 'Do you want to eat some more, too, Ray?'

'Not hungry any more,' the boy beside her replied. He was gazing out at the barbed-wire fench that streamed back outside the turned-up window.

'How far's it to Cape Town, Mummy?' Zaida asked, munching a sandwich.

'We'll be there tomorrow afternoon,' the woman said.

'Will Papa be waiting?'

'Of course.'

'There's some sheep,' the boy, Ray, said. A scattering of farm buildings went by, drab, domino-shaped structures along a brown slope.

The mother had been driving all night and she was fatigued, her eyes red, with the feeling of sand under the lids, irritating the eyeballs. They had stopped for a short while along the road, the night before; parked in a gap off the road outside a small town. There had been nowhere to put up for the night: the hotels were for Whites only. In fact, only Whites lived in these towns and everybody else, except for the servants, lived in tumbledown mud houses in the locations beyond. Besides, they did not know anybody in this part of the country.

Dawn had brought depression, gloom, ill-temper, which she tried to control in the presence of the children. After having parked on that stretch of road until after midnight, she had started out again and driven, the children asleep, through the rest of the night.

Now she had a bad headache, too, and when Zaida said, 'Can I have a meatball, Mummy?' she snapped irritably: 'Oh, dash it all! It's there, eat it, can't you?'

The landscape ripped by, like a film being run backwards, red-brown, yellow-red, pink-red, all studded with sparse bushes and broken boulders. To the east a huge outcrop of rock strata rose abruptly from the arid earth, like a titanic wedge of purple-and-lavender-layered cake topped with chocolate-coloured boulders. The car passed over a stretch of gravel road and the red dust boiled behind it like a flame-shot smoke-screen. A bird, its long, ribbon-like tail streaming behind it, skimmed the brush beyond the edge of the road, flitting along as fast as the car.

'Look at that funny bird, Mummy,' the boy, Ray, cried, and pressed his face to the dust-filmed glass.

The mother ignored him, trying to relax behind the wheel, her feet moving unconsciously, but skilfully, on the pedals in the floor. She thought that it would have been better to have taken a train, but Billy had written that he'd need the car because he had a lot of contacts to visit. She hoped the business would be better in the Cape. Her head ached, and she drove automatically. She was determined to finish the journey as quickly as possible.

Ray said, 'I want some coffee.' And he reached for the thermos flask on the rack under the dashboard. Ray could take care of himself, he did not need to have little things done for him.

'Give me some, too,' Zaida called from the back, among the suitcases.

'Don't be greedy,' Ray said to her. 'Eating, eating, eating.'

'I'm not greedy. I want a drink of coffee.'

'You had coffee this morning.'

'I want some more.'

'Greedy. Greedy.'

'Children,' the mother said wearily, 'children, stop that arguing.'

'He started first,' Zaida said.

'Stop it. Stop it,' the mother told her.

Ray was unscrewing the cap of the thermos. When it was off he drew the cork and looked in. 'Man, there isn't any,' he said. 'There isn't any more coffee.'

'Well, that's just too bad,' the mother said.

'I want a drink,' Zaida cried. 'I'm thirsty, I want some coffee.'

The mother said wearily: 'Oh, all right. But you've got to wait. We'll get some somewhere up the road. But wait, will you?'

The sun was a coppery smear in the flat blue sky, and the countryside, scorched yellow and brown, like an immense slice of toast, quivered and danced in the haze. The woman drove on, tiredly, her whole mind rattling like a stale nut. Behind the sunglasses her eyes were red-rimmed and there was a stretched look about the dark, handsome, Indian face. Her whole system felt taut and stretched like the wires of a harp, but too tight so that a touch might snap any one of them.

The miles purred and growled and hummed past: flat country and dust-coloured *koppies*, the baked clay *dongas* and low ridges of hills. A shepherd's hut, lonely as a lost soul, crouched against the shale-covered side of a flat hill; now and then a car passed theirs, headed in the opposite direction, going north, crashing by in a shrill whine of slip-stream. The glare of the sun quivered and quaked as if the air was boiling.

'I want some coffee,' Zaida repeated petulantly. 'We didn't have no coffee.'

'We'll buy some coffee,' her mother told her. 'We'll buy some for the road as soon as we get to a café. Stop it, now. Eat another sandwich.'

'Don't want sandwich. Want coffee.'

A group of crumbling huts, like scattered, broken cubes passed them in a hollow near the road and a band of naked, dusty brown children broke from the cover of a sheep-pen, dashing to the side of the road, cheering and waving at the car. Ray waved back, laughing, and then they were out of sight. The wind-scoured metal pylon of a water-pump drew up and then disappeared too. Three black men trudged in single file along the roadside, looking ahead into some unknown future, wrapped in tattered, dusty blankets, oblivious of the heat, their heads shaded by the ruins of felt hats. They did not waver as the car spun past them but walked with fixed purpose.

The car slowed for a steel-slung bridge and they rumbled over the dry, rock-strewn bed of a stream. A few sheep, their fleeces black with dust, sniffed among the boulders, watched over by a man like a scarecrow.

At a distance, they passed the coloured location and then the African location, hovels of clay and clapboard strewn like discoloured dice along a brown slope, with tiny people and ant-like dogs moving among them. On another slope the name of the town was spelled out in whitewashed boulders.

The car passed the sheds of a railway siding, with the sheep milling in corrals, then lurched over the crossing and bounced back on to the roadway. A Coloured man went by on a bicycle, and they drove slowly past the nondescript brown front of the Railway Hotel, a line of stores, and beyond a burnt hedge a group of white men with red, sun-skinned, wind-honed faces sat drinking at tables in front of another hotel with an imitation Dutch-colonial façade. There was other traffic parked along the dusty, gravel street of the little town: powdered cars and battered pick-up trucks, a wagon in front of a feed store. An old Coloured man swept the pavement in front of a shop, his reed broom making a hissing sound, like gas escaping in spurts.

Two white youths, pink-faced and yellow-haired, dressed in khaki shirts and shorts, stared at the car, their eyes suddenly hostile at the sight of a dark woman driving its shiny newness, metal fittings factory-smooth under the film of road dust. The car spun a little cloud behind it as it crept along the red-gravel street.

'What's the name of this place, Mummy?' the boy, Ray, asked.

'I don't know,' the mother replied, tired, but glad to be able to slow down. 'Just some place in the Karroo.'

'What's the man doing?' Zaida asked, peering out through the window.

'Where?' Ray asked, looking about. 'What man?'

'He's gone now,' the little girl said. 'You didn't look quickly.' Then, 'Will we get some coffee now?'

'I think so,' the mother said. 'You two behave yourselves and there'll be coffee. Don't you want a cool drink?'

'No,' the boy said. 'You just get thirsty again, afterwards.'

'I want a lot of coffee with lots of sugar,' Zaida said.

'All right,' the mother said. 'Now stop talking such a lot.'

Up ahead, at the end of a vacant lot, stood a café. Tubular steel chairs and tables stood on the pavement outside, in front of its shaded windows. Its front was decorated with old Coca Cola signs and painted menus. A striped awning shaded the tables. In the wall facing the vacant space was a foot-square hole where non-Whites were served, and a group of ragged Coloured and African people stood in the dust and tried to peer into it, their heads together, waiting with forced patience.

The mother drove the car up and brought it to a stop in front of the café. Inside a radio was playing and the slats of the venetian blinds in the windows were clean and dustless.

'Give me the flask,' the mother said, and took the thermos bottle from the boy. She unlatched the door. 'Now, you children, just sit quiet. I won't be long.'

She opened the door and slid out and, standing for a moment on the pavement, felt the exquisite relief of loosened muscles. She straightened body. But her head still ached badly and that spoiled the momentary delight which she felt. With the feeling gone, her brain was tired again and the body once more a tight-wound spring. She straightened the creases out of the smart tan suit she was wearing but left the jacket unbuttoned. Then, carrying the thermos flask, she crossed the sidewalk, moving between the plastic-and-steel furniture into the café.

Inside, the café was cool and lined with glass cases displaying cans and packages like specimens in some futuristic museum.

From somewhere at the back of the place came the smell and sound of potatoes being fried. An electric fan buzzed on a shelf and two gleaming urns, one of tea and the other of coffee, steamed against the back wall.

The only other customer was a small white boy with tow-coloured hair, a face like a near-ripe apple and a running nose. He wore a washed-out print shirt and khaki shorts, and his dusty bare feet were yellow-white and horny with cracked callouses. His pink, sticky mouth explored the surface of a lollipop while he scanned the covers of a row of outdated magazines in a wire rack.

Behind the glass counter and a trio of soda fountains a broad, heavy woman in a green smock thumbed through a little stack of accounts, ignoring the group of dark faces pressing around the square hole in the side wall. She had a round-shouldered, thick body and reddish-complexioned face that looked as if it had been sand-blasted into its component parts: hard plains of cheeks and knobbly cheek-bones and a bony ridge of nose that separated twin pools of dull grey; and the mouth a bitter gash, cold and malevolent as a lizard's, a dry, chapped and serrated pink crack.

She looked up and started to say something, then saw the colour of the other woman and, for a moment, the grey pools of the eyes threatened to spill over as she gaped. The thin pink mouth writhed like a worm as she sought for words.

'Can you fill this flask with coffee for me, please?' the mother asked.

The crack opened and a screech came from it, harsh as the sound of metal rubbed against stone. 'Coffee? My Lord Jesus Christ!' the voice screeched. 'A bedamned *coolie* girl in here!' The eyes started in horror at the brown, tired, handsome Indian face with its smart sunglasses, and the city cut of the tan suit. 'Coolies, Kaffirs and Hottentots outside,' she screamed. 'Don't you bloody well know? And you talk *English*, too, hey!'

The mother stared at her, startled, and then somewhere inside her something went off, snapped like a tight-wound spring suddenly loose, jangling shrilly into action, and she cried out with disgust as her arm came up and the thermos flask hurtled at the white woman.

'Bloody white trash!' she cried. 'Coolie yourself!'

The flask spun through the air and, before the woman behind the counter could ward it off, it struck her forehead above an eyebrow, bounced away, tinkling as the thin glass inside the metal cover shattered. The woman behind the counter screeched and clapped a hand to the bleeding gash over her eye, staggering back. The little boy dropped his lollipop with a yelp and dashed out. The dark faces at the square hatch gasped. The dark woman turned and stalked from the café in a rage.

She crossed the sidewalk, her brown face taut with anger and opened the door of her car furiously. The group of non-Whites from the hole in the wall around the side of the building came to the edge of the vacant lot and stared at her as she slammed the door of the car and started the motor.

She drove savagely away from the place, her hands gripping the wheel tightly, so that the knuckles showed yellow through the brown skin. Then she recovered herself and relaxed wearily, slowing down, feeling tired again, through her anger. She took her time out of town while the children gazed, sensing that something was wrong.

Then the boy, Ray, asked, 'Isn't there any coffee, Mummy? And where's the flask?'

'No, there isn't any coffee,' the mother replied. 'We'll have to do without coffee, I'm afraid.'

'I wanted coffee,' the little girl, Zaida, complained.

'You be good,' the mother said. 'Mummy's tired. And please stop chattering.'

'Did you lose the flask?' Ray asked.

'Keep quiet, keep quiet,' the woman told him, and they lapsed into silence.

They drove past the edge of the town, past a dusty service station with its red pumps standing like sentinels before it. Past a man carrying a huge bundle of firewood on his head, and past the last buildings of the little town: a huddle of whitewashed cabins with chickens scrabbling in the dooryard, a sagging shearing-shed with a pile of dirty bales of wool inside, and a man hanging over a fence, watching them go by.

The road speared once more into the yellow-red-brown countryside and the last green trees dwindled away. The sun danced and jiggled like a midday ghost across the expressionless earth, and the tyres of the car rumbled faintly on the black asphalt. There was some traffic ahead of them but the woman did not bother to try to overtake.

The boy broke the silence in the car by saying, 'Will Papa take us for drives?'

'He will, I know,' Zaida said. 'I like this car better than Uncle Ike's.'

'Well, *he* gave us lots of rides,' Ray replied. 'There goes one of those funny birds again.'

'Mummy, will we get some coffee later on?' Zaida asked.

'Maybe, dear. We'll see,' the mother said.

The dry and dusty landscape continued to flee past the window on either side of the car. Up ahead the sparse traffic on the road was slowing down and the mother eased her foot on the accelerator.

'Look at that hill,' the boy, Ray, cried. 'It looks like a face.'

'Is it a real face?' Zaida asked, peering out.

'Don't be silly,' Ray answered. 'How can it be a real face? It just *looks* like a face.'

The car slowed down and the mother, thrusting her head through her window, peered forward past the car in front and saw the roadblock beyond it.

A small riot-van, a Land Rover, its windows and spotlight screened with thick wire mesh, had been pulled up half-way across the road, and a dusty automobile parked opposite to it, forming a barrier with just a car-wide space between them. A policeman in khaki shirt, trousers and flat cap leaned against the front fender of the automobile and held a Sten-gun across his thighs. Another man in khaki sat at the wheel of the car, and a third policeman stood by the gap, directing the traffic through after examining the drivers.

The car ahead slowed down as it came up to the gap, the driver pulled up and the policeman looked at him, stepped back and waved him on. The car went through, revved and rolled away.

The policeman turned towards the next car, holding up a hand, and the mother driving the car felt the sudden pounding of her heart. She braked and waited, watching the khaki-clad figure strolling the short distance towards her.

He had a young face, with the usual red-burned complexion of the land, under the shiny leather bill of the cap. He was smiling thinly but the smile did not reach his eyes which bore the hard quality of chips of granite. He wore a holstered pistol at his waist and, coming up, he turned towards the others and called, 'This looks like the one.'

The man with the Sten-gun straightened but did not come forward. His companion inside the car just looked across at the woman.

The policeman in the road said, still smiling slightly: 'Ah, we have been waiting for you. You didn't think they'd phone ahead, hey?'

The children in the car sat dead still, staring, their eyes troubled. The mother said, looking out: 'What's it all about?'

'Never mind what's it all about,' the policeman said to her. '*You* know what it's all about.' He looked her over and nodded. '*Ja*, darkie girl with brown suit and sunglasses. You're under arrest.'

'What's it all about?' the woman asked again. Her voice was not anxious, but she was worried about the children.

'Never mind. You'll find out,' the policeman told her coldly. 'One of those agitators making trouble here. Awright, listen.' He peered at her with flint-hard eyes. 'You turn the car around and don't try no funny business, hey? Our car will be in front and the van behind, so watch out.' His voice was cold and threatening.

'Where are you taking us? I've got to get my children to Cape Town.'

'I don't care about that,' he said. 'You make trouble here then you got to pay for it.' He looked back at the police car and waved a hand. The driver of the police car started it up and backed and then turned into the road.

'You follow that motor car,' the policeman said. 'We're going back that way.'

The woman said nothing but started her own car, manoeuvring it until they were behind the police car.

'Now don't you try any funny tricks,' the policeman said again. She stared at him and her eyes were also cold now. He went back to the riot-truck and climbed in. The car in front of her put on speed and she swung behind it, with the truck following.

'Where are we going, Mummy?' asked Zaida.

'You be quiet and behave yourselves,' the mother said, driving after the police car.

The countryside, red-brown and dusty, moved past them: the landscapes they had passed earlier now slipping the other way.

The flat blue sky danced and wavered and the parched, scrub-strewn scenery stretched away around them in the yellow glare of the sun.

'I wish we had some coffee,' the little girl, Zaida, said.

The story is based on a true account given to me by an Asiatic South African woman who made a trip by car with her children from Johannesburg to Cape Town. She was let off by the police with a 'warning'. Having made the trip myself at some time or other, I was able to portray the journey and the scenery as it appears in the story. — Alex La Guma

ARTHUR C. CLARKE

Reunion

People of Earth, do not be afraid. We come in peace — and why not? For we are your cousins; we have been here before.

You will recognize us when we meet, a few hours from now. We are approaching the solar system almost as swiftly as this radio message. Already, your sun dominates the sky ahead of us. It is the sun our ancestors and yours shared ten million years ago. We are men and women as you are; but you have forgotten your history, while we have remembered ours.

We colonized Earth, in the reign of the great reptiles, who were dying when we came and whom we could not save. Your world was a tropical planet then, and we felt that it would make a fair home for our people. We were wrong. Though we were masters of space, we knew so little about climate, about evolution, about genetics. . .

For millions of summers — there were no winters in those ancient days — the colony flourished. Isolated though it had to be, in a universe where the journey from one star to the next takes years, it kept in touch with its parent civilization. Three or four times in every century, starships would call and bring news of the galaxy.

But two million years ago, Earth began to change. For ages it had been a tropical paradise; then the temperature fell, and the ice began to creep down from the poles. As the climate altered, so did the colonists. We realize now that it was a natural adaptation to the end of the long summer, but those who had made Earth their home for so many generations believed that they had been attacked by a strange and repulsive disease. A disease that did not kill, that did no physical harm — but merely disfigured.

Yet some were immune; the change spared them and their children. And so, within a few thousand years, the colony had split into two separate groups — almost two separate species — suspicious and jealous of each other.

The division brought envy, discord, and, ultimately, conflict. As the colony disintegrated and the climate steadily worsened, those who could do so withdrew from Earth. The rest sank into barbarism.

We could have kept in touch, but there is so much to do in a universe of a hundred trillion stars. Until a few years ago, we did not know that any of you had survived. Then we picked up your first radio signals, learned your simple languages, and discovered that you had made the long climb back from savagery. We come to greet you, our long-lost relatives — and to help you.

We have discovered much in the eons since we abandoned Earth. If you wish us to bring back the eternal summer that ruled before the Ice Ages, we can do so. Above all, we have a simple remedy for the offensive yet harmless genetic plague that afflicted so many of the colonists.

Perhaps it has run its course — but if not, we have good news for you. People of Earth, you can rejoin the society of the universe without shame, without embarrassment.

If any of you are still white, we can cure you.

R. T. KUROSAKA

A Lot to Learn

The Materializer was completed.

Ned Quinn stood back, wiped his hands, and admired the huge bank of dials, lights and switches. Several years and many fortunes had gone into his project. Finally it was ready.

Ned placed the metal skullcap on his head and plugged the wires into the control panel. He turned the switch to ON and spoke: 'Pound note.'

There was a whirring sound. In the Receiver a piece of paper appeared. Ned inspected it. Real.

'Martini,' he said.

A whirring sound. A puddle formed in the Receiver. Ned cursed silently. He had a lot to learn.

'A bottle of beer,' he said.

The whirring sound was followed by the appearance of the familiar brown bottle. Ned tasted the contents and grinned.

Chuckling, he experimented further.

Ned enlarged the Receiver and prepared for his greatest experiment. He switched on the Materializer, took a deep breath and said, 'Girl'.

The whirring sound swelled and faded. In the Receiver stood a lovely girl. She was naked. Ned had not asked for clothing.

She had freckles, a brace and pigtails. She was eight years old.

'Hell!' said Quinn.

Whirr.

The fireman found two charred skeletons in the smouldering rubble.

JANE ROGERS

True Romance

First Look

1. At last, across the crowded room, he managed to catch her eye. She gazed back at him, arrested, beautiful and unselfconscious as a wild creature facing a man; curious, but entirely other. She was lovely, and he knew then he must have her. It was love at first sight.

2. I really can't remember.

First Kiss

1. She looked forward to Sunday all week, and time passed so slowly it seemed more like a year. But like all good things, it proved a day well worth waiting for. There was a gusty, fitful wind and brave silvery sunshine, with fleecy little clouds racing across the great bare sky. He was waiting for her at the gate, as he said he would be, and his stern tanned face broke into a wide smile as he saw her battling against the wind towards him. He helped her over the gate and they walked together along the clean-washed beach, leaning forward into the wind, breathless and laughing. There was no need to talk — they were together. He reached for her hand, and she allowed his to brush hers, then

teasingly drew it away. He glanced at her, her eyes were sparkling with delight. Light as a leaf in the wind she spun away from him across the sand, her laughter tinkling behind her — and danced down to the sea's edge. He started to move after her, then froze for a moment as his heart lurched to a sudden love for her, as she ran, abandoned as a child, towards the sea, her blonde hair streaming out behind her. As he watched she reached the water's edge and stopped, a tiny fearless figure facing the great blue ocean, as if unaware of, or defying, the dangers and terrors those deeps held. He yearned to protect that fearlessness, to guard that innocent trust; to stand with her, to face together that great hazardous sea.

With a sense of passionate urgency he ran towards her, and as he approached she seemed to sense him and she turned to meet him. He grasped her violently in his arms and bent his lips to hers in a kiss that ran through her lips and body like a fire, melting her to him, fusing them together, man and woman, one being, in the promise of love.

2. On Sunday we were supposed to be going for a walk. It was very windy. I didn't want to go, when it came to it; it looked cold, and I was sure we would run out of conversation. We couldn't agree on where to go, I knew the wind would be terrible on the beach, coming straight off the sea, and I wanted to go along the valley which was at least reasonably well sheltered. But he wanted the beach. Which is where we went in the end. I was right, the wind was fierce, the spray spattered on us like rain. He was very jokey and talkative to begin with, talking about a film he'd seen last night (on his own?) and making jokes about English summers. But going along that beach was hard work. You had to keep your head down and your eyes half closed to stop the sand getting in; lean at a forty-five degree angle forwards into the wind; and shout at the top of your voice if you wanted to be heard above the roaring and crashing. I was wearing my anorak and it blew up with air so that I must have looked like a walking Michelin man. I just couldn't think of anything to say. Every now and then I could feel he was looking at me, so I'd look back at him and he'd give a smile or else look away quickly, so in the end I felt awkward and didn't know where to look.

After a bit he started talking, asking me things, I could hardly hear a word and had to keep screaming 'What?' and pointing to my ears to show I couldn't hear. He was asking me about my family and how long we'd lived here. Deliberately thinking of things to keep a conversation going. I wanted to say, if he must talk, why not go up further over the sand dunes so we'd be more protected? But I felt embarrassed to suggest it — couples go in the dunes — and anyway it would have meant we'd *have* to talk. When he gave up for a minute I ran off in front of him, partly to escape the next 'what?', partly because I was beginning to feel such a lump, plodding along. It would look as if I was enjoying it. I was, in a way, but it felt so awkward. I could have cheerfully run on, away, at full speed. He came running after me so I really put a spurt on, but he caught up with me in the end — grabbed my arm and I fell over on the sand. He leant over close to pull me up but instead of letting myself be pulled up I grabbed at his hands and pulled him sideways, so that he stumbled and fell heavily. I got up and stood laughing at him. But I felt awkward. I'd been too violent. I must have seemed like a silly kid — horse play. Was he trying to pull me towards him? I felt completely embarrassed, and started walking on. He caught up with me but didn't say anything. We walked back most of the way in silence. When we got to where the track meets the beach he stopped, poking a shell around with his toe in the sand. Then he picked it up again and said, 'Look.' I went to take it from him and he grabbed my hand. 'What?' I said, feeling foolish. I wished he'd get on with it, I could feel myself going red. He pulled me near and kissed my mouth, then he let go my hand and put his arm round my neck. He was pressing my head to him. He didn't just kiss me, he kept his mouth there, I couldn't breathe. I pushed at his chest and he drew back looking at me in surprise. I laughed, to excuse myself, and ducked under his arm and started to run up the beach. He would think I was stupid, I didn't know what to do. I wanted him to kiss me — I suppose I did — but not — I didn't know what I was supposed to do. Should I have taken my mouth away to breathe then kissed him back? I thought it would look as if I was too eager. I couldn't bear him to know no one had kissed me before.

Every time I thought of it afterwards I went hot with embarrassment; he would think I was a kid.

First Morning

1. *He bent over her sleeping head and whispered,*
'*I love you.' She stirred softly, and reached out her arms. Then she opened her eyes slowly and smiled at him. They embraced again.*

'*I'm so happy,' she said.*

'*You look like a fluffy little bird,' he whispered, stroking his hand over her rumpled curls. 'My little nest bird!' Gently, he kissed her lips, her eyes, her cheeks, pulled her tight to him again. 'I could stay here forever.' She turned her bright head away from him suddenly — 'Look! It's snowed!' He raised his head to look. Excited as a lovely child she jumped out of bed and ran to the window, and clapped her hands.*

'*It's deep! It's perfectly white everywhere — oh look!'*

Rapt, she stared out. He gazed at her profile, pure as a marble statue in the reflected snow light. She turned to him. 'It's for us,' she said. He looked puzzled. 'It's like a new world — everything clean and beautiful, all the dirt and ugliness is covered up, a beautiful white sparkling world — a world for lovers — our new world!' Moved, he got up and went to stand by her. Together they looked out at the dazzling unfamiliar scene.

'*We must go out!' she exclaimed. Turning to him, pleading as she saw his expression. 'Just for a little, just to run around and make some footprints. To show we know it's for us!' What a creature of impulse she was! She would be lovely in the snow, but standing here warm beside him, she was even lovelier. He pulled her more closely to him. 'Come back to bed first,' he breathed, in a voice thick with desire. With a mysterious little smile playing at the corners of her mouth, she tilted back her head and surveyed him. She was Cleopatra, mistress of love's secrets, artful. Then as suddenly she was close to him again, surrendered, loving, abandoned in her generosity. He carried her to the bed, watching her precious, familiar ever-new face, entranced; she was all women; like a beautifully cut diamond her many magical sides sparkled and complimented each other. This everchanging love could never end. Burying his face in her hair, he said softly,*

'*I love you. I love you.' Raising his head thoughtfully for a moment, speaking almost despite himself, he whispered to the white snow-lit room, 'It's the real thing.'*

2. It didn't seem as if I'd slept but I must have done because I opened my eyes and it was very light in the room — it was white. The light seemed unnatural, glaring. My eyes were watering like an old woman's. I turned my head and I could see his shoulder and hair. Carefully, I lifted up the bedclothes and got out of bed. He didn't move. I felt as if I would crack when I moved my legs apart. Very quietly I opened the door and went to the bathroom. The first thing I did was look in the mirror. I half expected — I don't know — to see a different face. At least to see that it had registered somewhere. I expected to look sensual, or experienced, or something. But the same blank face faced me. All its expressions were peeled off and it didn't tell me a thing. It didn't look secretive either. I went to the toilet and then I noticed the blood on my thigh, a thick black smear, dried. My stomach went tight. I started rubbing at it, then I wet some toilet paper and rubbed and scrubbed till it had gone, leaving a red scratched patch on my leg. I filled the sink and washed myself between the legs. It was sore.

When I'd finished I sat on the edge of the bath with the towel around me, I was cold but I didn't want to move. I felt as if I couldn't do anything. I wanted a mother or someone like that to take charge. What happens next? What when he wakes up? I wanted to be alone. I couldn't bear him to look at me till I knew what I was. I was like someone who's had an accident; they don't feel anything for a while, they're numb. I tried to think about it. But I felt nothing. I told myself, 'You've done it at last, you're like everyone else now. The barrier's down.' I tried to laugh at that, but my stone face refused to move. I didn't want to think over the details of it. 'You were glad when it was finished,' I told myself. That must be wrong. I didn't like it. It seemed like nothing.

I remembered I'd read about a custom in a tribe somewhere — in Africa, I expect. Just before a girl is married they keep her away from all the men, in a hut with her mother and all women relatives, and they prepare her. The night before the wedding they have a great feast and dance, with masks and music, a great ritual, the bride dances among the women and the music gets more and more frenzied, beating and beating, and at the climax the headman — with them all watching — he does it to her with a stick, a special kind of stick. And they all sing and celebrate when he shows the blood. They all rejoice. Then her women take her back and clean her and help her, and she meets her husband the next day, without that awful virginity between them. When I read it, it revolted me. Now I wish it had happened to me. Now I wish it had happened to me. It wouldn't be like nothing then; it would really be something.

I noticed the whitish light again and knelt on the toilet seat and lifted up the mucky net curtain to look out. It had snowed — everywhere was covered in white. I started to cry. It was utterly still out there, everything buried under thick snow, and the sky seemed low, deep grey; nothing moved. The whole world had changed in the night. I didn't want to be alone there. I thought we would be together. I did feel pleased in a way, that I'd done it — just because I had, like smoking your first cigarette. But it should be more than that. I was ashamed of my thought, because it made me even more separate from him. The tears kept rolling down my cheeks. I could keep them going, it was soothing. I stopped suddenly. I could see myself. *Wanting* to feel sad. I wasn't sad. I didn't feel anything.

I stay very still now, kneeling, looking out. My head is empty, I stare at the white snow and think nothing and feel nothing except the stillness.

I stare at it till my eyes are full of whiteness, my head is full of whiteness like a million empty pages; it doesn't matter, it hasn't even happened. Nobody knows it's happened except me, maybe it didn't even happen. What would make it real? Nobody knows, it's nothing. Nothing can matter; nothing matters to me. I am snow.

But I imagine him. The ice cracks. I see what he might see. Wondering where I am, coming quietly to the door and listening, then pushing it open slightly. Seeing me kneeling there with the towel round me looking out at the snow. I can see the picture he would see, the narrow brown shoulders and slipping towel and pink feet sticking out soles upwards. The separate captive creature staring out. His heart would melt. He'd come and put his arms around me. He would love my singleness. Yes!

I am posing.

When I went back to the bedroom I was nearly blue with cold but I felt fairly controlled. It was as if I'd put a great distance or age between myself and it. But he was still asleep! I could hardly believe that, it seemed to deny that I existed. I got dressed.

As I was putting my shoes on he woke up. 'Are you up already?'

'Yes.'

'Oh.' I stood for a moment waiting as if my feet were touching a crack in the ice. Say 'Come here', say 'I love you', say 'Are you all right?' He didn't say anything. I went to the window quickly, but my face was burning because he watched me walk.

'It's snowed.'

'Has it?'

'Yes.' Silence. Suddenly he sat up violently and said:

'I'm starving, it always makes me hungry. Let's go and buy some stuff to cook a big breakfast. Pass my jeans — on that chair.'

I couldn't believe it. 'It always makes me hungry.' While he got dressed I kept looking out the window. But he didn't even notice. He went to the door. 'Are you coming?' He started to go downstairs. He was behaving as if nothing had happened. Well? Nothing had happened.

But I felt frightened, as if I'd thrown something away without knowing its value. I remembered that he'd never even said 'I love you'. I'd been cheated.

This is the first story I ever had published in a real magazine, and for that reason it has always been special to me. I wrote it when I was twenty, and still working out of my system my anger at the way love (amongst other things!) is simplified and made sugary in women's magazines, and, more generally, in many stories and songs. But looking back now, I can see that I was also doing something else which has been important to me as a writer: this story is built upon a very simple structure of contrasts and so is similar to the structure of both my published novels, which are written in chapters presenting different characters' points of view. In this story I was evolving a way of writing which worked for me.

The other thing I like about the story is the way the romanticized version nearly works, in places; it brings back memories of avidly reading romance stories as a teenager, and longing to believe them, and almost being able to — whilst another part of my head knew they were nothing but sentimental rubbish.

— Jane Rogers

KATE CHOPIN

The Story of an Hour

Knowing that Mrs Mallard was afflicted with a heart trouble, great care was taken to break to her as gently as possible the news of her husband's death.

It was her sister Josephine who told her, in broken sentences; veiled hints that revealed in half concealing. Her husband's friend Richards was there, too, near her. It was he who had been in the newspaper office when intelligence of the railroad disaster was received, with Brently Mallard's name leading the list of 'killed'. He had only taken the time to assure himself of its truth by a second telegram, and had hastened to forestall any less careful, less tender friend in bearing the sad message.

She did not hear the story as many women have heard the same, with a paralyzed inability to accept its significance. She wept at once, with sudden, wild abandonment, in her sister's arms. When the storm of grief had spent itself she went away to her room alone. She would have no one follow her.

There stood, facing the open window, a comfortable, roomy armchair. Into this she sank, pressed down by a physical exhaustion that haunted her body and seemed to reach into her soul.

She could see in the open square before her house the tops of trees that were all aquiver with the new spring life. The delicious breath of rain was in the air. In the street below a peddler was crying his wares. The notes of a distant song which some one was singing reached her faintly, and countless sparrows were twittering in the eaves.

There were patches of blue sky showing here and there through the clouds that had met and piled one above the other in the west facing her window.

She sat with her head thrown back upon the cushion of the chair, quite motionless, except when a sob came up into her throat and shook her, as a child who has cried itself to sleep continues to sob in its dreams.

She was young, with a fair, calm face, whose lines bespoke repression and even a certain strength. But now there was a dull stare in her eyes, whose gaze was fixed away off yonder on one of those patches of blue sky. It was not a glance of reflection, but rather indicated a suspension of intelligent thought.

There was something coming to her and she was waiting for it, fearfully. What was it? She did not know; it was too subtle and elusive to name. But she felt it, creeping out of the sky, reaching toward her through the sounds, the scents, the color that filled the air.

Now her bosom rose and fell tumultuously. She was beginning to recognize this thing that was approaching to possess her, and she was striving to beat it back with her will — as powerless as her two white slender hands would have been.

When she abandoned herself a little whispered word escaped her slightly parted lips. She said it over and over under her breath: 'free, free, free!' The vacant stare and the look of terror that had followed it went from her eyes. They stayed keen and bright. Her pulses beat fast, and the coursing blood warmed and relaxed every inch of her body.

She did not stop to ask if it were or were not a monstrous joy that held her. A clear and exalted perception enabled her to dismiss the suggestion as trivial.

She knew that she would weep again when she saw the kind, tender hands folded in death; the face that had never looked save with love upon her, fixed and gray and dead. But she saw beyond that bitter moment a long procession of years to come that would belong to her absolutely. And she opened and spread her arms out to them in welcome.

There would be no one to live for her during those coming years; she would live for herself. There would be no powerful will bending hers in that blind persistence with which men and women believe they have a right to impose a private will upon a fellow-creature. A kind intention or a cruel intention made the act seem no less a crime as she looked upon it in that brief moment of illumination.

And yet she had loved him — sometimes. Often she had not. What did it matter! What could love, the unsolved mystery, count for in face of this possession of self-assertion which she suddenly recognized as the strongest impulse of her being!

'Free! Body and soul free!' she kept whispering.

Josephine was kneeling before the closed door with her lips to the keyhole, imploring for admission. 'Louise, open the door! I beg; open the door — you will make yourself ill. What are you doing, Louise? For heaven's sake open the door.'

'Go away. I am not making myself ill.' No; she was drinking in a very elixir of life through that open window.

Her fancy was running riot along those days ahead of her. Spring days, and summer days, and all sorts of days that would be her own. She breathed a quick prayer that life might be long. It was only yesterday she had thought with a shudder that life might be long.

She arose at length and opened the door to her sister's importunities. There was a feverish triumph in her eyes, and she carried herself unwittingly like a goddess of Victory. She clasped her sister's waist, and together they descended the stairs. Richards stood waiting for them at the bottom.

Someone was opening the front door with a latchkey. It was Brently Mallard who entered, a little travel-stained, composedly carrying his grip-sack and umbrella. He had been far from the scene of accident, and did not even know there had been one. He stood amazed at Josephine's piercing cry; at Richards' quick motion to screen him from the view of his wife.

But Richards was too late.

When the doctors came they said she had died of heart disease — of joy that kills.

PATRICK O'BRIAN

Samphire

Sheer, sheer, the white cliff rising, straight up from the sea, so far that the riding waves were nothing but ripples on a huge calm. Up there, unless you leaned over, you did not see them break, but for all the distance the thunder of the water came loud. The wind, too, tearing in from the sea, rushing from a clear, high sky, brought the salt tang of the spray on their lips.

They were two, standing up there on the very edge of the cliff: they had left the levelled path and come down to the break itself and the man was crouched, leaning over as far as he dared.

'It *is* a clump of samphire, Molly,' he said; then louder, half turning, 'Molly, it *is* samphire. I *said* it was samphire, didn't I?' He had a high, rather unmasculine voice, and he emphasized his words.

His wife did not reply, although she had heard him the first time. The round of her chin was trembling like a child's before it cries: there was something in her throat so strong that she could not have spoken it if it had been for her life.

She stepped a little closer, feeling cautiously for a firm foothold, and she was right on him and she caught the smell of his hairy tweed jacket. He straightened so suddenly that he brushed against her. 'Hey, look out,' he said, 'I almost trod on your foot. Yes, it *was* samphire. I said so as soon as I saw it from down there. Have a look.'

94

She could not answer, so she knelt and crawled to the edge. Heights terrifed her, always had. She could not close her eyes; that only made it worse. She stared unseeing, while the brilliant air and the sea and the noise of the sea assaulted her terrified mind and she clung insanely to the thin grass. Three times he pointed it out, and the third time she heard him so as to be able to understand his words. '. . . fleshy leaves. You see the fleshy leaves? They used them for pickles. Samphire pickles!' He laughed, excited by the wind, and put his hand on her shoulder. Even then she writhed away, covering it by getting up and returning to the path.

He followed her. 'You noted the *fleshy leaves*, didn't you, Molly? They allow the plant to store its nourishment. Like a cactus. Our *native* cactus. I *said* it was samphire at once, didn't I, although I have never actually seen it before. We could almost get it with a stick.'

He was pleased with her for having looked over, and said that she was coming along very well: she remembered — didn't she? — how he had had to persuade her and persuade her to come up even the smallest cliff at first, how he had even to be a little firm. And now there she was going up the highest of them all, as bold as brass; and it was quite a dangerous cliff too, he said, with a keen glance out to sea, jutting his chin; but there she was as bold as brass looking over the top of it. He had been quite right insisting, hadn't he? It was worth it when you were there, wasn't it? Between these questions he waited for a reply, a 'yes' or hum of agreement. If he had not insisted she would always have stayed down there on the beach, wouldn't she? Like a lazy puss. He said, wagging his finger to show that he was not quite in earnest, that she should always listen to her Lacey (this was a pet name that he had coined for himself). Lacey was her lord and master, wasn't he? Love, honour, and obey?

He put his arm round her when they came to a sheltered turn of the path and began to fondle her, whispering in his secret night-voice, Tss-tss-tss, but he dropped her at once when some coast-guards appeared.

As they passed he said, 'Good day, men,' and wanted to stop to ask them what they were doing but they walked quickly on.

*   *   *

In the morning she said she would like to see the samphire again. He was very pleased and told the hotel-keeper that she was becoming quite the little botanist. He had already told him and the nice couple from Letchworth (they were called Jones and had a greedy daughter: he was an influential solicitor, and Molly would be a clever girl to be nice to them), he had already told them about the samphire, and he had said how he had recognized it at once from lower down, where the path turned, although he had only seen specimens in a *hortus siccus* and illustrations in books.

On the way he stopped at the tobacconist on the promenade to buy a stick. He was in high spirits. He told the man at once that he did not smoke, and made a joke about the shop being a house of ill-*fume*; but the tobacconist did not understand. He looked at the sticks that were in the shop but he did not find one for his money and they went out. At the next tobacconist, by the pier, he made the same joke to the man there. She stood near the door, not looking at anything. In the end he paid the marked price for an ash walking-stick with a crook, though at first he had proposed a shilling less: he told the man that they were not ordinary summer people, because they were going to have a villa there.

Walking along past the pier towards the cliff path, he put the stick on his shoulder with a comical gesture, and when they came to the car park where a great many people were coming down to the beach with picnics and pneumatic rubber toys he sang, 'We are the boys that nothing can tire; we are the boys that gather samphire.' When a man who was staying in the same hotel passed near them, he called out that they were going to see if they could get a bunch of jolly good samphire that they had seen on the cliff yesterday. The man nodded.

It was a long way to the highest cliff, and he fell silent for a little while. When they began to climb he said that he would never go out without a stick again; it was a fine, honest thing, an ashplant, and a great help. Didn't she think it was a great help? Had she noticed how he had chosen the best one in the shop, and really it was very cheap, though perhaps they had better go without tea tomorrow to make it up. She remembered, didn't she, what they had agreed after their discussion about an exact allowance for every day? He was walking a few feet ahead of her, so that each time he had to turn his head for her answer.

It was blowing harder than the day before on the top, and for the last hundred yards he kept silent, or at least she did not hear him say anything.

At the turn of the path he cried, 'It is still there. Oh jolly good. It is still there, Molly,' and he pointed out how he had first seen the samphire, and repeated, shouting over the wind, that he had been sure of it at once.

For a moment she looked at him curiously while he stared over and up where the plant grew on the face of the cliff, the wind ruffling the thin, fluffy hair that covered his baldness, and a keen expression on his face; and for a moment she wondered whether it was perhaps possible that he saw beauty there. But the moment was past and the voice took up again its unceasing dumb cry: Go on, oh, go on, for Christ's sake, go on, go on, go on, oh go *on*.

They were there. He had made her look over. 'Note the fleshy leaves,' he had said; and he had said something about samphire pickle! and how the people at the hotel would stare when they brought it back. That was just before he began to crouch over, turned from her so that his voice was lost.

He was leaning right over. It was quite true when he said that he had no fear of heights: once he had astonished the workmen on the steeple of her uncle's church by walking among the scaffolding and planks with all the aplomb of a steeplejack. He was reaching down with his left arm, his right leg doubled under him and his right arm extended on the grass: his other leg was stretched out along the break of the cliff.

*   *   *

Once again there was the strong grip in her throat; her stomach was rigid and she could not keep her lip from trembling. She could hardly see, but as he began to get up her eyes focused. She was already there, close on him — she had never gone back to the path this time. God give me strength, but as she pushed him she felt her arms weak like jelly.

Instantly his face turned; absurd, baby-face surprise and a shout unworded. The extreme of horror on it, too. He had been half up when she thrust at him, with his knee off the ground, the stick hand over and the other clear of the grass. He rose, swaying out. For a second the wind bore his body and the stick scrabbled furiously for a purchase on the cliff. There where the samphire grew, a little above, it found a hard ledge, gripped. Motionless in equilibrium for one timeless space — a cinema stopped in action — then his right hand gripped the soil, tore, ripped the grass and he was up, from the edge, crouched, gasping huge sobbing draughts of air on the path.

He was screaming at her in an agonized falsetto interrupted by painful gasps, searching for air and life. 'You pushed me, Molly you — pushed me. You — pushed me.'

She stood silent, looking down and the voice rushed over her. You pushed — you pushed me — Molly. She found she could swallow again, and the hammering in her throat was less. By now his voice had dropped an octave: he had been speaking without a pause but for his gasping — the gasping had stopped now, and he was sitting there normally. '. . . not well; a spasm. Wasn't it, Molly?' he was saying; and she heard him say 'accident' some-times.

Still she stood, stone-still and grey and later he was saying '. . . *possibly* live together? How can we *possibly* look at one another? After this?' And some time after it seemed to her that he had been saying something about their having taken their room for the month . . . accident was the word, and spasm, and not well — fainting? It was, wasn't it, Molly? There was an unheard note in his voice.

She turned and began to walk down the path. He followed at once. By her side he was, and his face was turned to hers, peering into her face, closed face. His visage, his whole face, everything, had fallen to pieces: she looked at it momentarily — a very old terribly frightened comforting-itself small child. He had fallen off a cliff all right.

He touched her arm, still speaking, pleading, 'It *was* that, wasn't it, Molly? You didn't push me, Molly. It was an accident . . .'

She turned her dying face to the ground, and there were her feet marching on the path; one, the other; one, the other; down, down, down.

Most people will agree that a really happy marriage is a very rare thing; indeed, if they look about among their acquaintances they may not find one wholly contented pair for forty or fifty ill-matched couples who should never have come together. I was reflecting upon this state of affairs as I walked along the cliffs that overhang the sea near our house, and a striking example occurred to me — that of a particularly elegant, intelligent woman who in her extreme and utterly inexperienced youth had married a bore, or at least a man who had developed into a bore, a didactic eternally prating bore. At some point in my walk I noticed some plants growing quite far down on the rock-face: the lines about the samphire-gatherer in King Lear *drifted into my mind, and as I walked on in a vague, musing state, the two notions combined and this tale took shape without any conscious effort on my part.*

That, as far as my experience goes, is how short stories and poems usually arise: a novel, of course, is quite a different thing.
— Patrick O'Brian

RUKSHANA SMITH

Sumitra

The hall was hushed. Sumitra lifted the guitar, pushed her long hair behind her back, strummed an introduction and began to sing. Her voice rang out clear and sweet, the audience hung on every word. In the front row a woman sobbed with emotion.

As the song ended the audience rose with one accord, cheering and applauding wildly. Sumitra bowed, turned to walk off the stage, but they would not let her go. 'Sing it again!' they yelled. 'More, more!' She smiled and began to play another tune.

'Belt up, Sumitra,' shouted Sandya from the next room, banging crossly on the wall. 'I'm trying to do my homework!' Mai was calling up the stairs, 'Come and help me, stop playing that guitar. I wish Martin had never given it to you!' Sumitra closed her eyes as the anger spluttered like a fire-cracker inside her. The vision of headlines reading: 'Sue Patel Takes New York by Storm! Beautiful Girl Singer from London, England, an Overnight Success!' faded, and she strummed three angry chords before throwing the guitar on her bed. She went downstairs to exchange the sweet smell of success for the acrid fumes of boiling *ghee*.

As she fried the rounds her mother rolled out, a huge wave of misery engulfed her. Hilary and Lynne had gone to a local college dance, while Cinderella Patel remained at home, reeking of oil and dry flour. She turned suddenly and looked at Mai. 'Do you like cooking?' she asked, wondering how her mother could bear this life, day after day. Mai was bewildered. 'What questions you

100

ask!' she replied. 'I don't know. Women cook for their families.
You must help me and learn to cook for your own family. You are
sixteen. Soon we must start thinking about looking for a husband.
It is good you have passed your exams. You will marry well!'

Sumitra's tongue stuck to her mouth like an uncooked lump of
dough. She turned the *poori* deftly as her mind screamed, 'Never,
never, never!' in the kitchen of her brain. The words of a pop song
sizzled in the fat:

'And all the songs I was going to sing, I'll never sing them now.
And all the bells I was going to ring, I'll never ring them now.
And all the lives I was going to live
And all the loves I was going to give
I'll never live them now
I'll never give them now.'

Mai patted her arm, leaving a floury impression like a palm
print decorating a temple. 'It's all right,' she said with unusual
gentleness. 'It is the custom. You'll get used to the idea, there's no
need to be shy. We all get used to it.'

It had never occurred to Mai that her daughters might be
questioning their way of life. Despite their smart clothes and the
fact that at the weekends they wore sweaters and jeans like any
other teenager, she was sure that their attitudes and conventions
were Indian. She had never sat down and thought about it; she
never thought about her children as separate entities. When she
told Bap that she was worried about them, she meant that she
was concerned that they would take suitable jobs, choose the
right friends, marry decent partners. The criterion in each case
was whether or not she would approve of their choice. So Mai
was part of the Banquo line, carefully bequeathing to her children
the ideas and philosophies that had been bequeathed to her. The
fact that these conventions had evolved in different ages and in
different countries was immaterial.

Mai never doubted that the girls would lead their lives in the
same way as she lived hers, marrying someone carefully chosen
by the parents, bearing children who would, of course, speak
Gujarati and Hindi. She had no reason to doubt it when all
around her she saw other cultures passing on their various truths
to their own children and carefully isolating them from the
British tradition in which they lived. She had seen synagogues,

mosques, Greek and Russian orthodox churches, and behind each of these institutions was a sub-culture energetically devoted to keeping a particular tradition alive.

Mai, like thousands of other mothers of minority groups, had many ways of perpetuating tradition. There was emotional, social and financial pressure. Thus the little dictatorships of family life flourished in the British democracy. Children were unhappy, rejected their parents' demands temporarily, made their heroic gestures, but were usually defeated by the sanctions imposed. Mothers wept, fathers talked of sacrifices, grandparents disapproved, and the son or daughter conceded and was sucked back into the family group.

Life continued as it had always done. The shrine was cleaned and polished, sandalwood paste prepared. Offerings were left for the gods and roses decorated the ceremonial place. The girls plaited Gopal and Jayant braids at Rakshabandan in order to ensure their health and happiness. They all went to the temple and, occasionally, to Indian films and dances.

As long as the outside culture remained beyond her house, Mai was content. The letters and notes from the alien society were ignored as if they had no right to be there. Requests to attend school functions or parents' evenings were left unanswered. What could she or Bap do at school? She trusted the teachers to do their job and, besides, she couldn't speak English. So she lived in her comfortable cocoon, only venturing out to go to work and surrounding herself with the friends she had known in Uganda.

Sumitra and some of her Indian friends, however, were beginning to resent the tight community laws. They objected to being relegated to the Bottom Division at the back of the temple. As sexual objects women distracted the men from their prayers, so the men prayed while the women sat behind the barrier and gossiped. Then the women went to the communal kitchen to prepare food for the men. This division of labour annoyed the girls, who at school were encouraged to be independent, thoughtful, integrated, and at home to be docile, submissive and dutiful. Sumitra had to listen to the adults decrying the British way of life, while being educated into it herself.

Sumitra and her parents lived under the same roof without speaking to each other. Of course they talked; they spoke about the things that did not matter, but about the serious business of the meaning of life they were silent. There was no point of contact, and any questioning was called disobedience and would cause a scene. So Sumitra acted one part at home and another at school, and was never sure which role was really hers.

Sometimes events on the news reached out and touched them. Incidents of growing racial tension in Notting Hill, Birmingham, Southall. The places were different but the causes were the same: a lack of Government awareness and initiative and an unfriendly host population causing the immigrants to turn in on themselves. One side felt threatened, the other rebuffed.

Sumitra felt all these pressures. One part of her wanted to live as an Indian girl, carrying on the great traditions and culture, while another part of her wanted to participate in Western freedom. On the one hand they read of incidents in Southall, of young Asians being attacked and even murdered. This made them fearful, retreating into the group. These racial incidents defined certain boundaries between the minority groups and host society, and caused Bap to give his weekly lecture on the superiority of their own way of life.

On the other hand there were occasionally reports in the paper about young Asian girls killing themselves because they had not wanted to go through with an arranged marriage, or because the strain of living two lives was overwhelming. As she watched yet another *poori* puff up and turn brown, Sumitra wondered if that was the only way out. She had often wished lately that she was dead.

The next morning Sumitra work early from a restless sleep and lay in bed dully staring at the cracked plaster patterns on the ceiling. She heard squeals and thumps as Ela and Bimla chased each other round their bedroom. The sunlight fell through the curtain. Sumitra closed her eyes. The thought of life closing around her was stifling. She felt once more like a figure in a glass bubble, shaken in all directions by some huge hand that controlled her future.

A car hooted outside. 'Shut up! Go away and leave me alone!' she shouted. The doorbell rang. Muttering angrily, she pulled on some clothes and went downstairs. Ela had already opened the door, and Martin, Maria and Sally were standing in the front hall.

'Come on!' Martin said. 'Hurry up and get ready! It's a beautiful day and we're going to Littlehampton.' Ela dashed off to tell Mai. 'I'm so glad to see you,' Sumitra beamed. 'I'll make coffee and get some food together.' She bustled round happily wrapping food in paper bags, while Sally related the fight she had had with Ben at nursery.

They piled into the car, Mai with Sally on her lap, Maria squashed between Ela and Bimla. Bap stayed at home, glad of a peaceful day. The bank holiday traffic was heavy and Martin's car overheated so they had to keep stopping, but they laughed and joked and sang their way to the coast.

Finding a sheltered spot on the beach, they unpacked the picnic. As usual when they all went out, there was a mixture of English and Indian food. Egg sandwiches, *chapattis*, tomato rolls, *pooris*, crisps, *chevra*, *samosas*, and bread-pudding. The young children ran about collecting stones and sea-shells. Sandya paddled in the sea, the wind blowing her dress against her thin figure, like one of Lowry's matchstick ladies. Sumitra tucked up her jeans and went to join her. She felt warm, contented and at peace. Martin strode off into the distance making for the headland.

Maria grinned at Mai. 'It's lovely, isn't it? I love the seaside. I said to Martin we should all go out today.'

'Fine.' Mai smiled back.

Maria put her hand on to the sand. She lifted her fingers and watched the golden grains trickle out. 'Do you know what this is called?'

'I don't know.'

'Sand,' said Maria. 'Sand,' repeated Mai. Maria picked up a shell. 'Shell,' she said. 'Shell,' Mai repeated. Maria sighed. 'I really must start giving you English lessons once a week.' Despite her intentions she still hadn't got round to keeping her promise. She had bought a book for teaching English to foreign students, but with the excitement of the wedding, it still lay unopened in its wrapper. 'I'll start next week.'

Mai smiled. She closed her eyes. It felt good sitting in the warmth and feeling the sun shining on her. It was like Uganda with the sea glistening and the children playing around them.

Sumitra and Sandya ran back, laughing and shaking cold water over them. They flopped on the sand. 'Any food left?' asked Sumitra. 'I'm starving!' 'I wish we'd brought a ball,' said Ela, running up. 'I've got one somewhere in this bag,' said Maria, rummaging through her basket. They all played football until Martin came back, windswept and his face burnt by the sun.

'Come on, we're off!' he announced. 'No, no!' squealed the little girls. 'Not yet, we've only just come!' 'We're going on a speedboat,' he laughed. 'Of course, if you don't want to come . . .' The rest of the sentence was drowned in whoops of joy. He led them down to the pier, running ahead with the younger children, while Sandya and Sumitra gazed in shop windows and Mai and Maria followed sedately.

Mai hung back from the boat. 'Come on!' Maria insisted, pulling her arm, 'it's lovely.' 'I no like,' Mai faltered. 'Come on, Mai,' said Sandya. Mai sat gingerly on one of the seats, pulling her sari tightly around herself. Maria sat next to her, holding her arm. The wind tore through their hair, the spray stung their eyes. The boat lifted its prow to the wind, racing through the water. No sooner had the ride finished, than Ela cried, 'Can we have another go, Mai, please?' 'Of course you can't,' scolded Sandya. 'Don't be so greedy!' Mai looked in her purse. It was good to see the girls enjoying themselves so much. 'You want again? Bimla, Maria, Sandya?' They shook their heads and disembarked.

'Here, Sumitra, take her round again.' Mai gave her the money.

'You ought to get a season ticket,' commented the boatman as he swung the boat away. 'Hold on.'

The two girls clasped the rail. Sumitra willed the boat to go faster — the speed was exhilarating and mind-deadening. It was impossible to feel worried or tense with the air whipping her cheeks and hair flying around her face. Closing her eyes she let her tensions be swept away by the wind.

It was funny how different things seemed. Yesterday everything was difficult and dreary. Now, because Martin had taken them out for the day, nothing seemed the same. It was a matter of perspective. When they went up the Thames on an outing things changed depending on where she was standing: looking down at a boat from a bridge, or looking across from the banks, or on the boat waving at people on the riverside. Yet she was the same person no matter where she stood.

Now she was conscious of the others watching her and Ela from the shore. Glancing through her lids against the salt spray, she felt her little sister's warm hand in hers and could just make out the laughing group on the quayside, waiting for the boat to come in. *If only I could stay here for ever*, she thought, *whizzing round and round in increasing circles, never reaching land.* The boat dropped speed and slowed in to moor. Ela squeezed her fingers. 'Wasn't that terrific!'

Ela dashed up the steps to Bimla. 'That was great, even better than the first time! You should have come.' Turning to Maria she said, 'Bimla's scared. She was scared on the plane, and she's scared of boats too. She's a real coward!'

'I'm not a coward!' Bimla retaliated indignantly. 'You should see Ela when we come out of school. She hides behind me when the boys call us names!'

They all began walking into town. Maria stopped to fasten Sally's anorak; Ela and Bimla waited with her. 'What do you mean? Who calls you names?'

'The boys from Finchley Down.'

'What do they call you?' Maria asked.

'Oh just, you know, things like Paki, and Blackie, and stuff like that.'

Maria stopped walking and Sally tugged impatiently at her hand. 'That's awful,' said Maria. 'Doesn't anyone tell them off?'

'Once a man told them off, but usually nobody seems to hear.'

'Martin's got a friend who works at Finchley Down. I'll ask him to see what he can do about it.' They ran to catch up with the others. They trooped into the town and headed for Mario's coffee bar. Martin ordered coffee, cakes and ice cream. Mai looked happy and carefree, Ela and Bimla were tired and laughing, Sandya and Sumitra were busy teasing Martin. Sally spread chocolate cream all round her face, and Mai wiped it off with a tissue.

'We're like a big family,' Maria thought, 'all different types and ages, but all bound together by a bond of affection.'

She grinned to herself. 'What are you laughing at?' asked Martin. Maria smiled at him. Sumitra felt a pang of envy as she saw the understanding glance they exchanged. They were so happy; she was glad for Maria's sake, but although Maria always told her that nothing had changed, she was always welcome, somehow their togetherness emphasized her own isolation.

Bimla stuffed the rest of her éclair into her mouth. 'Don't forget it's my birthday next week!' she reminded them, scattering crumbs all over the table. 'You better eat a bit slower or you'll choke before then!' said Martin. 'Anyway, we couldn't forget,' added Maria, 'you've been reminding us for months!'

Sumitra had ordered a cake from the shop around the corner and she and Mai had been busily baking biscuits and mounds of food. Motiben, Leela, Jayant and little Trupti were coming too.

On Sunday, Sumitra and Sandya set the food out in the lounge. The cake proclaimed in blue icing, HAPPY BIRTHDAY, BIMLA. Motiben and the rest of the family arrived soon after lunch and gave Bimla her presents. Ela pressed her face to the window, looking for Martin's car. 'Here they are!' she yelled as it came down the street. Maria waved as she and Sally carried out brightly wrapped parcels from the boot.

Bimla and Ela rushed to the door. 'Come in, come in!' Bimla urged. 'Jayant bought me a desk and Sumitra got me some pens and a birthday cake and Sandya gave me a pencil case and Ela made me a cat out of felt and Mai . . .'

'Let them come in first!' laughed Sandya, coming up behind and rescuing them from one of Bimla's unending sentences. 'Come in and sit down. You know everyone, don't you?' They went into the lounge. Sally toddled up to the loaded table and grabbed a sandwich. Maria caught her up and led her away. 'Wait until you're asked,' she said.

Bimla opened her parcels. There was a painting book from Sally and some oil paints from Maria. Martin produced an easel. Bimla hugged her friends. 'Thanks, thank you. I really wanted some paints and an easel. Mrs Johnson says I should be an artist. I think I will, too.' Mai and Sumitra handed round the food, and they all sat on the floor eating and talking. The birthday candles were lit. Sally pulled Mai over to the window. 'Curtains. Must pull curtains, like at nursery.' Mai pulled the curtains and they sang 'Happy Birthday' in English and Gujarati, and cheered as Bimla blew out the candles.

'Good, good,' said Jayant, throwing Ela into the air. 'You are getting big too, aren't you?' Bap put on some Indian records and they sat round tapping their feet. Sumitra sat down on the floor near Maria. 'Isn't it your birthday soon, Sumitra?' asked Leela. 'You'll be seventeen, won't you? What are you going to do?'

'She's coming to work in my shop,' Jayant said. 'There's a job ready for her.'

Jayant's shop was in a busy road in Edgware. He sold sweets, cigarettes and magazines, and needed another pair of hands. Sumitra looked at her parents. 'I want to stay on at school,' she mumbled, embarrassed. 'I'm not sure what I'm going to do yet.' One thing she was sure about. She was not going to work for Jayant. She was going to be an air-hostess, but had not yet mentioned this at home. She had talked about it to her friends at school but until she knew what qualifications were necessary she had no intention of seeing her plans squashed. Her parents would be delighted if she worked with Jayant but Sumitra wanted something wider than that for herself. She wanted to step outside her daily routine and see new things, meet new people.

'Sumitra ought to stay at school,' Maria supported her. 'If she does A-levels, she'll have more opportunities open to her.'

'Opportunities, opportunities,' scoffed Jayant. 'She is a woman. What does she want opportunities for? All she needs is a husband. I am offering her a good job till she finds one.'

Maria caught Sumitra's eye. What Jayant was telling her was to mind her own business.

Sally saved the moment of awkward silence by pouring her orange juice over Trupti. Trupti howled. Maria dashed out to get a cloth and the moment passed. But Sumitra knew that this was only a temporary respite. Mai had already spoken of her marriage openly. She and Bap were looking forward to the day when they would see their eldest daughter settled and that in turn would open the way for Sandya. So although no one referred to the subject of her future again, it was there and facing up to it was inescapable.

When she had waved goodbye to the last of the guests and tucked a happy and exhausted Ela into bed, Sumitra retreated to her room. She picked up her guitar and another song formed itself in her mind. It spoke of sadness and joy, of excitement and duty, of those she knew and loved and of those she was yet to meet. She called it 'Sumitra'.

Sumitra and her family came to England from Uganda in 1970. We met in a hostel for the homeless and became close friends. This story describes Sumitra's growing realization that adulthood brings both freedom and constraints. Her parents assume that she will continue their traditions, while Sumitra has ambitions and wishes of her own. — Rukshana Smith

LIAM O'FLAHERTY

The Sniper

In 1922, after the war between Ireland and England, a treaty was written naming six counties in the North of Ireland which would come under British rule. The people of Ireland were divided about whether or not to accept such a treaty; after the war many wanted peace above all else. As a result, families were split into those 'pro' and those 'anti' the treaty; those who wanted partition were called the Free Staters, those who wanted a united Ireland were called Republicans.

In Dublin the anti-treaty forces had taken control of the area surrounding a building called 'The Four Courts' and were defending it against the pro-treaty forces. This story takes place in this area of Dublin. — Editors

The long June twilight faded into night. Dublin lay enveloped in darkness, but for the dim light of the moon, that shone through fleecy clouds, casting a pale light as of approaching dawn over the streets and the dark waters of the Liffey. Around the beleaguered Four Courts the heavy guns roared. Here and there through the city machine guns and rifles broke the silence of the night, spasmodically, like dogs barking on lone farms. Republicans and Free Staters were waging civil war.

On a roof-top near O'Connell Bridge, a Republican sniper lay watching. Beside him lay his rifle and over his shoulders were slung a pair of field-glasses. His face was the face of a student — thin and ascetic, but his eyes had the cold gleam of the fanatic. They were deep and thoughtful, the eyes of a man who is used to looking at death.

He was eating a sandwich hungrily. He had eaten nothing since morning. He had been too excited to eat. He finished the sandwich, and taking a flask of whiskey from his pocket, he took a short draught. Then he returned the flask to his pocket. He paused for a moment, considering whether he should risk a smoke. It was dangerous. The flash might be seen in the darkness and there were enemies watching. He decided to take the risk. Placing a cigarette between his lips, he struck a match, inhaled the smoke hurriedly and put out the light. Almost immediately, a bullet flattened itself against the parapet of the roof. The sniper took another wiff and put out the cigarette. Then he swore softly and crawled away to the left.

Cautiously he raised himself and peered over the parapet. There was a flash and a bullet whizzed over his head. He dropped immediately. He had seen the flash. It came from the opposite side of the street.

He rolled over the roof to a chimney stack in the rear, and slowly drew himself up behind it, until his eyes were level with the top of the parapet. There was nothing to be seen — just the dim outline of the opposite housetop against the blue sky. His enemy was under cover.

Just then an armoured car came across the bridge and advanced slowly up the street. It stopped on the opposite side of the street fifty yards ahead. The sniper could hear the dull panting of the motor. His heart beat faster. It was an enemy car. He wanted to fire, but he knew it was useless. His bullets would never pierce the steel that covered the grey monster.

Then round the corner of a side street came an old woman, her head covered by a tattered shawl. She began to talk to the man in the turret of the car. She was pointing to the roof where the sniper lay. An informer.

The turret opened. A man's head and shoulders appeared, looking towards the sniper. The sniper raised his rifle and fired. The head fell heavily on the turret wall. The woman darted toward the side street. The sniper fired again. The woman whirled round and fell with a shriek into the gutter.

Suddenly from the opposite roof a shot rang out and the sniper dropped his rifle with a curse. The rifle clattered to the roof. The sniper thought the noise would wake the dead. He stopped to pick the rifle up. He couldn't lift it. His forearm was dead. 'Christ,' he muttered, 'I'm hit.'

Dropping flat on to the roof, he crawled back to the parapet. With his left hand he felt the injured right forearm. The blood was oozing through the sleeve of his coat. There was no pain — just a deadened sensation, as if the arm had been cut off.

Quickly he drew his knife from his pocket, opened it on the breastwork of the parapet and ripped open the sleeve. There was a small hole where the bullet had entered. On the other side there was no hole. The bullet had lodged in the bone. It must have fractured it. He bent the arm below the wound. The arm bent back easily. He ground his teeth to overcome the pain.

Then, taking out his field dressing, he ripped open the packet with his knife. He broke the neck of the iodine bottle and let the bitter fluid drip into the wound. A paroxysm of pain swept through him. He placed the cotton wadding over the wound and wrapped the dressing over it. He tied the end with his teeth.

Then he lay still against the parapet, and closing his eyes he made an effort of will to overcome the pain.

In the street beneath all was still. The armoured car had retired speedily over the bridge, with the machine gunner's head hanging lifeless over the turret. The woman's corpse lay still in the gutter.

The sniper lay for a long time nursing his wounded arm and planning escape. Morning must not find him wounded on the roof. The enemy on the opposite roof covered his escape. He must kill that enemy and he could not use his rifle. He had only a revolver to do it. Then he thought of a plan.

Taking off his cap, he placed it over the muzzle of his rifle. Then he pushed the rifle slowly upwards over the parapet, until the cap was visible from the opposite side of the street. Almost immediately there was a report, and a bullet pierced the centre of the cap. The sniper slanted the rifle forward. The cap slipped down into the street. Then, catching the rifle in the middle, the sniper dropped his left hand over the roof and let it hang, lifelessly. After a few moments he let the rifle drop to the street. Then he sank to the roof, dragging his hand with him.

Crawling quickly to the left, he peered up at the corner of the roof. His ruse had succeeded. The other sniper seeing the cap and rifle fall, thought that he had killed his man. He was now standing before a row of chimney pots, looking across, with his head clearly silhouetted against the western sky.

The Republican sniper smiled and lifted his revolver above the edge of the parapet. The distance was about fifty yards — a hard shot in the dim light, and his right arm was paining him like a thousand devils. He took a steady aim. His hand trembled with eagerness. Pressing his lips together, he took a deep breath through his nostrils and fired. He was almost deafened with the report and his arm shook with the recoil.

Then, when the smoke cleared, he peered across and uttered a cry of joy. His enemy had been hit. He was reeling over the parapet in his death agony. He struggled to keep his feet, but he was slowly falling forward, as if in a dream. The rifle fell from his grasp, hit the parapet, fell over, bounded off the pole of a barber's shop beneath and then cluttered on to the pavement.

Then the dying man on the roof crumpled up and fell forward. The body turned over and over in space and hit the ground with a dull thud. Then it lay still.

The sniper looked at his enemy falling and he shuddered. The lust of battle died in him. He became bitten by remorse. The sweat stood out in beads on his forehead. Weakened by his wound and the long summer day of fasting and watching on the roof, he revolted from the sight of the shattered mass of his dead enemy. His teeth chattered. He began to gibber to himself, cursing the war, cursing himself, cursing everybody.

He looked at the smoking revolver in his hand and with an oath he hurled it to the roof at his feet. The revolver went off with the concussion, and the bullet whizzed past the sniper's head. He was frightened back to his senses by the shock. His nerves steadied. The cloud of fear scattered from his mind and he laughed.

Taking the whiskey flask from his pocket, he emptied it at a draught. He felt reckless under the influence of the spirits. He decided to leave the roof and look for his company commander to report. Everywhere around was quiet. There was not much danger in going through the streets. He picked up his revolver and put it in his pocket. Then he crawled down through the skylight to the house underneath.

When the sniper reached the laneway on the street level, he felt a sudden curiosity as to the identity of the enemy sniper whom he had killed. He decided that he was a good shot whoever he was. He wondered if he knew him. Perhaps he had been in his own company before the split in the army. He decided to risk going over to have a look at him. He peered around the corner into O'Connell Street. In the upper part of the street there was heavy firing, but around here all was quiet.

The sniper darted across the street. A machine gun tore up the ground around him with a hail of bullets, but he escaped. He threw himself face downwards beside the corpse. The machine gun stopped.

Then the sniper turned over the dead body and looked into his brother's face.

JOHN WICKHAM

Meeting in Milkmarket

Thirty-five years ago George Sampeter and I sat in the same class next to each other in the elementary school. We were friends, by which I mean that he was easy with me and I liked him and was easy with him. You will see that I am using 'friends' in the sense in which I would have used it as a child, innocently and trustingly. Now, before I use the word, I must, as it were, look behind my back. I must ask myself whether the thing that exists deserves the name, whether I am not perhaps claiming too much. But I was less cautious when George and I walked together from school and shared sugar cakes and fish cakes and I did not question whether the thing that we shared could justify its claim to the title of friendship.

Today I met George in the Milkmarket after more than thirty years. The thing that strikes me now is my own reaction to meeting him after so long. From day to day I often see men who went to school with me and who have, in the common way of speaking, done well for themselves. They are now doctors and lawyers, some of them, politicians and high-up civil servants and one of them is the chief justice, a knight and counsel of the queen. Sometimes, depending on the propitiousness of the occasion, the time of day or night, the place and the surroundings, the degree of

114

sobriety, they see me too and nod a greeting or avert their eyes to a shop window as the case may be. Whenever I encounter one of these people I always feel a burning angry shame and self-contempt and invariably that day or night I contrive to get quite drunk. Nowadays I get drunk much too often. They know not what they do, these people. And this is why I am not afraid to say that George was my friend, is my friend, for seeing him has left me happy and glad in a choking way that I was at school with him, glad for myself and somehow simply and unambiguously rewarded by the memory that when we were children I shared in his life and experiences.

I remember very clearly the morning that George came to school for the first time. He was late and prayers had already been said when his father led him through the schoolroom to the headmaster's desk on the platform. I could see that he was frightened by the way he held on to his father's hand and I felt a trifle sorry for him that he needed a hand to clutch for support in what seemed to me no great ordeal. I think now that there was also in me a little envy of his fortune in having a father's hand to clutch. The headmaster greeted George's father warmly and it was clear that they were friends and that George would be one of those boys who would get special treatment, being the son of the head's friend. That made me angry, I remember. What made me even more angry was that George was put straight into the second standard. This seemed a monstrous piece of favouritism. But it did not last long. By the next morning George was among us humbler folk in the first standard: he could read very well and on this basis had been put into the class above but the teacher soon found out that George couldn't do sums and so, according to the rule which counted skill at sums as superior to all other skills, George had to be demoted. They put him to sit next to me. He was crying from the public shame. I wanted to comfort him but I could think of no way of doing it. He had a new slate and a new pencil which for some reason would not write. I had an old cigarette tin full of pencil ends (in all my school days I never had a whole pencil) and I gave him one and showed him how to lick the tip with his tongue to make it write. We became friends from that moment and I have never ceased to be proud of myself for that simple gesture. I have done nothing in my life since, which has pleased me more.

George came from the country and brought with him a sense of wonder and thrill at the sights of town. Our school was a slum school in the heart of the dirty back streets, littered with fruit skins, reeking with the 'fainty-fainty' smell of rotten and rotting fruit. In the doorways of Suttle Street the patois-speaking *mesdames* from Dominica and St Lucia watched over barrels of mangoes and sacks of charcoal. All sorts of spices spread a perfume in the air and the girls of the town, their mouths filled with gold and curses, slutted and strutted along the narrow wet street. George loved it all. I did not, I lived in it. After school every afternoon I would try to persuade George to take the road by way of the waterfront so that we might look at the schooners and the barebacked seamen smoking on the decks or fishing over the sides: the smell of the sea offered a more promising and certainly cleaner prospect than the one that hedged me around in Suttle Street. But the dirt and the muck fascinated George: the sacking curtains that screened the beds from the street, the smoky oil lamps, the half-starved dogs, kicked from one end of the road to the other. He would spend an hour listening to the patois shouts and curses that flew across the street and so miss his bus.

George in those days had a country boy's simplicity and lack of guile and I prided myself on my sharpness, my knowledge of the back streets and the ways of the city. I showed off to George and he rewarded me by finding everything I showed him fascinating.

My mother made our living by taking in washing and selling sugar cakes and fish cakes at the door of our house. As I have said, after school in the afternoon, I was always reluctant to take the road past our house on our way to George's bus. It is easy to say that I was ashamed and did not want George to see where I lived, but this would have been true only at first. It was more than that, I think Suttle Street was a dirty, filthy place. It was never clean. I lived there because I had no other place to live but I hated the place. But there was another reason for George's eagerness to pass by my house which I never suspected. It was my mother who told me one evening when I came home alone that she thought that he was fond of my sister Florianne. Like so many other facts, as soon as I had been told I recognised this as true beyond question and could not understand how I could have failed to see it before. George could draw very well and he was forever filling his drawing book with sketches of Florianne and asking me to

give them to her. As far as I remember, he never spoke more than
a few words to her when they met on the road before or after
school. Florianne went to the girls' school next to the church and
since this was on our way home, she had to dawdle to make sure
of meeting us. Others besides my mother had noticed it too and
very soon George became the victim of some very cruel teasing
from the boys which led, in the end, to the end of the affair, such
as it was.

I find it now very difficult to say all this. First of all, it happened
such a long time ago and then, although in my memory it seems
big and important and to contain the distillation of our time and
place, yet I have a misgiving that it is pitiably trivial and not
worth the weight which my own heart seems to give it. And yet I
know that I was right and that the trivial events of thirty years
ago opened my eyes to the realities. It has always amused me
when people refer to sexual and biological matters as the facts of
life and imply that the child who has been made aware of them is
no longer to be thought of as a child. But the true facts of life are
hardly so simple. The mating of male and female and the
resulting production of animal life, these in my experience hold
less mystery and need far less explanation than the conventions
and artificialities which we have erected to separate one person
from another. Yet no one explains or tries to explain these facts
of life to a child who is left to blunder against closed doors, to
fumble with false combinations and finally to wander forever in a
bewilderment from which neither age nor future experience ever
succeeds in rescuing him.

The teasing of the boys was not malicious, and yet I cannot be
sure. Perhaps, after all, it was more than a simple recital of the
facts and contained some recognition that any conceivable affection between George and my sister upset some sort of balance
and did not fit into a desirable scheme of things. It was not that
our schoolfellows were more than normally class conscious in
any crude way but they reacted in the only way they knew to an
incongruity which they recognised immediately. They laughed
and chanted: 'Georgie like a barefoot girl.' They saw no irony in
the fact that several of them wore no shoes themselves. They
repeated the chant at every opportunity until the simple fact
became a taunt, then an accusation, and then something like a
savage curse. I can hear it now, the ringing almost triumphant

'Georgie like a barefoot girl' as three or four boys trail behind
George and myself as we turn the corner by the church and the
girls' school. The words seem to tell the total story of our society.
They need no explanation, they stand by themselves as a monu-
ment to the crassness of human thinking, the grossness of our
sentiments and the thoughtless, awful cruelty of our behaviour.

'Georgie like a barefoot girl.' The chanted refrain echoes in my
memory and even now I can feel the helpless anger which flooded
through me. I was helpless but George was both helpless and
frightened. He had never experienced anything like it and his
patent terror made me take what action I could to help him —
action that showed how ignorant I was of the ways of the adult
world.

One morning George came as usual to wait for me while I got
myself ready for school. As he waited outside in the street while I
swallowed my breakfast biscuit, four boys turned the corner by
the grocery. George sensed that they would begin their usual
chant and tried to escape by diving into our front room. But he
could not escape and when I came out of the back room I found
him cornered like an animal while the four boys chanted the
usual words. My mother was not at home but Florianne was and
I could hear her sobs as she tried to stifle them by burying her
head in the bedclothes. George and I were followed all the way to
school by the cruel refrain.

I went straight to the headmaster, thinking in my innocence
that as he was the friend of George's father, he would at least find
some sort of suitable rebuke for the boys. What he did was much
simpler. He summoned George and told him that he must stop at
once his practice of walking along Suttle Street. There were other
roads, he said, decent roads which George could take. He also
told George's father some version of the story for, from the
following morning, someone accompanied George to school and
came in the afternoon to collect him. That was the end of our
walks through town, our idlings by the waterfront and the shop
windows, the end of something which had hardly begun but
which we had shared, the end of any promise which our
friendship had seemed to hold. It was not long after that George
left the elementary school and our paths ceased to cross.

Today it seems strange that in all the in-between years we never
so much as spoke to each other: we might just as well have been in

different worlds. I did see George some years after when he was about sixteen, playing cricket for his school. When he came to bat, my heart was in my mouth for him but he could not know that I was in the crowd. And then I heard that he had gone abroad and that was all.

Today he saw me before I saw him. His voice has not changed very much, it had always been deep. He shouted to me from the other side of the street and when I heard my name I turned to see him smiling. I was as pleased as a child, I can't say how pleased I was. He shook my hand and asked how I was. His voice was careful and controlled. I could not answer. My clothes, the shiny old trousers, spoke for themselves. He was confident, assured, in a sports shirt and light cotton slacks and open-toed sandals, like a tourist. It was good to see him and to be remembered by him. And then a cloud crossed his face and he said, 'Stanley, it's been a long time, I am glad to see you, but I must run.' 'Yes,' I said. I understood. He let go of my hand while he spoke and after he had left me I stood watching his figure mingle with the crowd in the Milkmarket.

But what I cannot understand is why, as he was leaving I should have said to him, to George, my friend, 'Goodbye, sir.'

Although the events of the story never occurred, they could well have. In that sense, the story is autobiographical. I wrote it while I was living in a small French town near Geneva and it is a reflection on my days at school and the great difference which a scholarship to a secondary school made between the lives of my schoolfellows, whom I remembered with affection, and my own.
— John Wickham

TONI CADE BAMBARA

Happy Birthday

Ollie spent the whole morning waiting. First she tried shaking Granddaddy Larkins, who just wouldn't wake up. She thought he was just playing, but he was out. His teeth weren't even in the glass, and there was a bottle on the bedstand. He'd be asleep for days. Then she waited on the cellar steps for Chalky, the building superintendent, to get through hauling garbage and come talk. But he was too busy. And then Ollie sat on the stairs waiting for Wilma. But it was Saturday and Wilma'd be holed up somewhere stuffing herself with potato chips and crunching down on jaw breakers, too greedy to cool it and eat 'em slow. Wilma'd come by tomorrow, though, and lie her behind off. 'I went to Bear Mountain yesterday on a big boat with my brother Chestnut and his wife,' she'd say, 'and that's why I didn't come by for you cause we left so early in the morning that my mother even had to get me up when it was still dark out and we had a great time and I shot bows and arrows when we got there, and do you like my new dress?' Wilma always had some jive tale and always in one breath.

Ollie tried to figure out why she was even friends with Wilma. Wilma was going to grow up to be a lady and marry a doctor and live in New York, Wilma's mother said. But Ollie, poor orphan, was going to grow up and marry a drinking man if she didn't get killed first, Wilma's mother said. Ollie never told Granddaddy

Larkins what Wilma's mother was all the time saying. She just hated her in private.

Ollie spent the early afternoon sitting on the rail in front of The Chicken Shack Restaurant, watching the cooks sling the wire baskets of chicken in and out of the frying fat. They were too sweaty and tired to tell her to move from in front. 'Ruining the business,' the owner used to fuss. Later she stood between the laundry and shoe store, watching some men pitch pennies against the building. She waited for a while, squeezing a rubber ball in her hand. If I can just get the wall for a minute, she thought, maybe somebody'll come along and we'll have us a good game of handball. But the men went right on pitching while other ones were waiting their turn. They'd be there for hours, so Ollie left.

She knocked on Mrs Robinson's door to see if she wanted her dog walked. It was cool in the hallway at least. No one was home, not even the loud-mouth dog that usually slammed itself against the door like he was big and bad instead of being just a sorry little mutt. Then Ollie took the stairs two at a time, swinging up past the fourth floor to the roof. There was rice all over. Ronnie must have already fed his pigeons. The door to the roof was unlocked, and that meant that the big boys were on the roof. She planted her behind against the door and pushed. She kicked at a cluster of rice. Some grains bounced onto the soft tar of the roof and sank. When Ollie moved onto the roof, the blinding sun made her squint. And there they were, the big boys, jammed between the skylight and the chimney like dummies in a window, just doing nothing and looking half-asleep.

Peter Proper, as always, was dressed to the teeth. 'I naturally stays clean,' he was always saying. Today he said nothing, just sitting. Marbles, a kid from the projects, had an open book on his knees. James was there, too, staring at a fingernail. And Ferman, the nut from crosstown, and Frenchie, the athlete. A flurry of cinders floated down from the chimney and settled into their hair like gray snow.

'Why don't you just sit in the incinerator? You can get even dirtier that way,' Ollie yelled. No one moved or said anything. She expected Frenchie to at least say, 'Here comes Miss Fresh-mouth,' or for Peter to send her to the store for eighteen cents' worth of American cheese. It was always eighteen cents' worth, and he always handed her a quarter and a nickel. Big Time. 'Don't none of you want nothing from the store today?' She squinted with her hands on her hips, waiting for the store dummies to start acting like Marbles, Peter, James, and so forth.

Ferman straightened out a leg against the skylight. 'Ollie, when are you going to learn how to play with dolls?'

'Ya want anything from the store, Ferman Fruitcake? I'm too big for dolls.' Ollie hitched up her jeans.

Ferman started to say something, but his audience was nearly asleep. Frenchie's head was nodding. James was staring into space. The pages of the open book on Marbles' knees were turning backward, three at a time, by themselves. Peter Proper was sitting very straight, back against the chimney with his eyes closed to the sun.

Ollie turned, looking over the edge of the roof. There was no one down in the park today. There was hardly anyone on the block. She propped a sticky foot against the roof railing and scraped off the tar. Everything below was gray as if the chimney had snowed on the whole block.

Chalky, the superintendent, was rolling a mattress onto a cart. Maybe he'd play cards with her. Just last Friday he had, but sometimes he wouldn't even remember her and would run and hide thinking she was King Kong come down just to hit him in the head or something. Ollie looked past the swings to the track. Empty. Frenchie should be out there trotting, she thought, looking back at him. He was dipping his head. Sometimes she'd trot beside Frenchie, taking big jumps to keep up. He'd smile at her but never teased her about them silly little jumps. He'd tell her for the hundredth time how he was going to enter the Olympics and walk off with a cup full of money.

'Go away, little girl!' Ferman had just yelled at her as if he had forgotten her name or didn't know her any more. He's as crazy as Chalky, thought Ollie, slamming the big roof door behind her and running down the stairs to the street. They must be brothers.

It was now four o'clock by the bank clock. Ollie remembered the bar-b-que place that had burned down. But she'd already rummaged through the ruins and found nothing. No use messing up her sneakers any further. She turned around to look the block over. Empty. Everyone was either at camp or at work or was sleeping like the boys on the roof or dead or just plain gone off.

She perched on top of the fire hydrant with one foot, balancing with her arms. She could almost see into the high windows of Mount Zion A.M.E. Church. 'This time I'm going to fly off and kill myself,' she yelled, flapping her arms. A lady with bundles turned the corner and gave Ollie a look, crossed against the traffic, looking over her shoulder and shaking her head at what the kids of today had come to. Reverend Hall came out of the church basement, mopping his head with a big handkerchief.

'You go play somewhere else,' he said, frowning into the sun.

'Where?' Ollie asked.

'Well, go to the park and play.'

'With who?' she demanded. 'I've got nobody to play with.'

Reverend Hall just stood there trying to control his temper. He was always chasing the kids. That's why he's got no choir, Granddaddy Larkins was always saying. He always chases kids and dogs and pigeons and drunks.

'Little girl, you can't act up here in front of the church. Have you no. . .'

'How come you always calling me little girl, but you sure know my name when I'm walking with my grandfather?' Ollie said.

'Tell'm all about his sanctified self,' said Miss Hazel, laughing out her window. But when the Reverend looked up to scowl, she ducked back in. He marched back into the church, shooing the pigeons off the steps.

'Wish me happy birthday,' Ollie whispered to the pigeons. They hurried off toward the curb. 'Better wish me happy birthday,' she yelled, 'or somebody around here is gonna get wasted.'

Miss Hazel leaned out the window again. 'What's with you, Ollie? You sick or something?'

'You should never have a birthday in the summertime,' Ollie yelled, 'cause nobody's around to wish you happy birthday or give you a party.'

'Well, don't cry, sugar. When you get as old as me, you'll be glad to forget all about . . .'

'I'm not crying.' Ollie stamped her foot, but the tears kept coming and before she could stop herself she was howling, right there in the middle of the street and not even caring who saw her. And she howled so loudly that even Miss Hazel's great-grandmother had to come to the window to see who was dying and with so much noise and on such a lovely day.

'What's the matter with the Larkins child?' asked the old woman.

'Beats me.' Miss Hazel shook her head and watched Ollie for a minute. 'I don't understand kids sometimes,' she sighed, and closed the window so she could hear the television good.

Follow On

The aim of all the activities in this section is to add to your enjoyment and understanding of the stories in this anthology. Some stories you may simply want to read and remember, others you may want to talk and write about, others may spark-off memories and further ideas.

The suggestions for activities fall into three broad areas:

Before reading — enabling you to anticipate and speculate about what is going to happen.

During reading — building up a picture of what is going on and what may happen next.

After reading — allowing time to reflect on the setting, events, characters, issues and themes within the stories; giving opportunities for discussion, and for personal, critical and discursive writing.

Many of the activities will involve a mixture of individual, group and whole class work. You may not want to attempt all of the suggested activities but choose ones which particularly interest you. In some cases you may wish to ignore them altogether and devise an activity or response of your own.

General activities

Before reading

▶ Read an extract, poem, play or short story which:
— takes up similar themes or issues
— presents characters/settings in similar/contrasting ways
— is written in a similar/contrasting style or genre.

▶ Take some general issues or questions raised in the story and discuss them in advance to find out how much you and others know and what opinions you have about them. After reading the story, discuss how far your ideas and opinions may have changed.

▶ Use the titles and/or the first few paragraphs to speculate and predict what the story may be about.

▶ Take some quotations from the story and speculate how the story will develop.

During reading

▶ Stop at various points during reading, and review what has happened so far, then predict what might happen next or how the story may develop.

▶ Stop at various points and discuss why writers have made certain decisions and what alternatives were open to them.

▶ Decide who is telling or speaking the story.

▶ Look out for important quotations that help reveal the meaning of the story.

▶ Makes notes and observations on plot, character, relationships between characters, style and the way the narrative works.

▶ Consider the various issues, themes or questions relating to the story which you discussed before reading.

▶ Build up a visual picture of the setting in order to work out its significance in the story or to represent it as a diagram.

After reading

▶ Discuss a number of statements about the story and decide which best conveys what the story is about.

▶ Prepare a dramatic reading of parts of the text.

▶ Use the story as a stimulus for personal and imaginative writing:
— writing stories/plays/poems on a similar theme
— writing stories/plays/poems in a similar style, genre or with a similar structure.

▶ Discuss and write imaginative reconstructions or extensions of the text:
— rewriting the story from another character's point of view
— writing a scene which occurs before the story begins
— continuing beyond the end of the story
— writing an alternative ending
— changing the narrative from the first to the third-person and vice versa
— experimenting with style and form
— picking a point in the story where the action takes a turn in direction and rewriting the rest of the story in a different way.

▶ Represent some of the ideas, issues and themes in the story for a particular purpose and audience:
— enacting a public inquiry or tribunal
— conducting an interview for TV or radio
— writing a newspaper report or press release
— writing a letter to a specified person or organisation
— giving an eye-witness report.

▶ Select passages from the story for film or radio scripting; act out the rehearsed script for a live audience, audio or video taping.

▶ Write critically or discursively about the story, or comparing one or more story, focusing on:
— the meaning of the title
— character, plot and structure
— style, tone, use of dialect, language
— build up of tension, use of climax, humour, pathos, etc.
— endings
— themes and issues.

Stories by themes

For readers wishing to examine particular themes through the stories, the checklist on the following page may be useful.

General issues raised in the anthology: ┌─► Pin Money
work; music; sexuality; women and ─────┼─► Nineteen Fifty-Five
men's rights; exploitation   └─► A Dangerous Influence

             ┌─► White Lies
Racism ─────────────────────┼─► Coffee for the Road
           └─┌► Reunion
Genre: science-fiction; romance ──────┼─► A Lot to Learn
           ┌─└► True Romance
Gender issues: marriage;   ├─► The Story of an Hour
teenage love   ├─► Samphire
Family relationships and divides: └─┌► Sumitra
different cultures; conflict ──────────└─► The Sniper

Autobiography: friendship; childhood ──┌► Meeting in Milkmarket
             └► Happy Birthday

▶ One theme running through almost all the stories — which students may wish to pursue — might be phrased as follows:
  'What do you do/when you can't do/what you want?'

Pin Money

Before reading

▶ What does the title suggest this story could be about?

▶ 'Pin Money' takes up a number of general issues like equal pay, unemployment, government subsidies for increasing employment opportunities. It also raises questions such as:
  — should trade union members engage in unofficial action?
  — do men have more right to work than women in times of unemployment?
  — what are the pros and cons of accepting voluntary redundancy?
  Discuss these questions before reading the story and find out what everyone in the group knows and thinks about them. After reading the story, discuss how far your ideas may have changed.

During reading

▶ Stop at the following points during reading and predict what is going to happen next:
  — at the *end* of the paragraph beginning, ' "Bloody radio." They always switched it on when . . .' (page 12)
  — after ' "Don't you worry Else. We'll stick up for you. We'll go to the union", said Winnie.' (page 15)

— after ' "Lock ourselves in the office where the machine button is . . . 'til they give Elsie 'er job back." ' (page 20)

— after 'Next morning they turned the radio to the local station and listened to the news of their sit-in.' (page 25)

— at the *end* of the paragraph beginning, 'Outside a group of men gathered.' (page 27).

▶ While you are reading, look out for the following:
— the arguments for and against the dismissal of one of the workers
— any phrases or sentences which seem important to you
— any terms which need further explanation: for example, the Equal Pay Act.

After reading

▶ In the story Tracey agrees to write a press release. Bearing in mind all the grievances the women have expressed and their reasons for deciding to have a sit-in, write a short statement (not more than 300 words) which clearly puts their case.

▶ The song 'Maintenance Engineer' takes up some of the women's arguments in 'Pin Money' and extends them. Using the ideas in both these pieces, and opinions you have yourself, write an essay titled 'Women's Work: Inside and Outside the Home'.

'Maintenance Engineer' by Sandra Kerr

(© Sandra Kerr. From *My Song Is My Own* © Frankie Armstrong, Kathy Henderson, Sandra Kerr, Alison McMorland, published by Pluto Press.)

One Friday night it happened, soon after we were wed,
When my old man came in from work as usual I said :
'Your tea is on the table, clean clothes are on the rack,
Your bath will soon be ready, I'll come up and scrub your back.'
He kissed me very tenderly and said, 'I'll tell you flat
The service I give my machine ain't half as good as that.'

I said . . .

Chorus

I'm not your little woman, your sweetheart or your dear
I'm a wage slave without wages, I'm a maintenance engineer.

Well then we got to talking. I told him how I felt,
How I keep him running just as smooth as some conveyor belt!
Well after all, it's I'm the one provides the power supply
He goes just like the clappers on me steak'n kidney pie.
His fittings are all shining 'cos I keep 'em nice and clean
And he tells me his machine tool is the best I've ever seen.

But . . .

Chorus

The terms of my employment would make your hair turn grey,
I have to be on call you see for 24 hours a day.
I quite enjoy the perks though while I'm working through the night
For we get job satisfaction. Well he does, and then I might.
If I keep up full production, I should have a kid or two,
So some future boss will have a brand new labour force to screw.

So . . .

Chorus

The truth began to dawn then, how I keep him fit and trim
So the boss can make a nice fat profit out of me and him.
And, as a solid union man, he got in quite a rage
To think that we're both working hard and getting one man's wage.
I said 'And what about the part-time packing job I do?
That's three men that I work for love, my boss, your boss and you.'

So . . .

Chorus

He looked a little sheepish and he said, 'As from today
The lads and me will see what we can do on equal pay.
Would you like a housewives' union? Do you think you should get paid?
As a cook and as a cleaner, as a nurse and as a maid?'
I said, 'Don't jump the gun love, if you did your share at home,
Perhaps I'd have some time to fight some battles of my own.'

For . . .

Chorus

I've often heard you tell me how you'll pull the bosses down.
You'll never do it brother while you're bossing me around.

'Til women join the struggle, married, single, white and black
You're fighting with a blindfold and one arm behind your back.'
The message has got over now for he's realised at last
That power to the sisters must mean power to the class.

And . . .

Chorus

Repeat: *I'm not your little woman, your sweetheart or your dear*
I'm a wage-slave without wages
I'm a maintenance engineer.

▶ Write an essay using the following quotation from 'Pin Money' as a
title: ' "A bloke needs a job. They get ever so down when they're out
of work. A woman's got plenty to occupy her but a man wouldn't
know what to do with himself stuck at 'ome all day." ' (page 13)

▶ This story ends unexpectedly and violently. Write about your view
on the ending. Before you begin, consider the following questions:
— Why do you think the writer chose to end her story in this way?
— What difference would it have made to the story as a whole if it
had ended two paragraphs before with the words 'late night radio
music'? (page 27)
— What other endings are possible? (You could offer an alternative
ending within this piece of writing.)

▶ In groups of 3 – 6 prepare, rehearse and tape a five minute slot for
the local radio 'News Round-up' programme covering the sit-in.
The programme would be co-ordinated by a radio presenter and
could include interviews/statements from the factory owner, a
union representative, men waiting at the gates and a phone call to
the women in the sit-in. (For ideas look at pages 25–26).

▶ Some weeks later, a public inquiry is called into the incidents leading
up to the factory break-in. Those represented at this inquiry are:
— the women
— the employers
— the union.
The inquiry is chaired by a panel of up to four 'impartial'
observers. In three groups representing the separate parties, prepare
your arguments and proposals. Remember that you will be able to
call on different characters in the story to put your case. The panel
should prepare a list of questions to ask the three parties and be

prepared to offer a workable resolution to the dispute at the end of the inquiry. When all the groups are thoroughly prepared, conduct the inquiry.

Nineteen Fifty-Five

Before reading

▶ Read the first section of this story down to, 'His hair is black and curly and he looks like a Loosianna creole.' (page 29) Now ask the following questions about it:
— where is the story set?
— what is learnt about the narrator of the story?
— why are the two men visiting her?
— what can be said about the way in which the story is written?
— how might the story develop?

During reading

▶ Write down any references you can find to real people and also any clues which link the characters in this story with real people and situations.

▶ Make a note of any points of style and structure which hold your attention. For example: words/phrases, changes in tense, use of punctuation, breaks in the story, use of memories and flashbacks.

After reading

It is interesting to look at the history of American music this century: Paul Whiteman was crowned 'King of Jazz', Benny Goodman the 'King of Swing', and Elvis Presley the 'King of Rock 'n' Roll'. All these men were white. The black originators and geniuses like Duke Ellington, Count Basie, Billie Holiday, Joe Turner and Little Richard have been denied true recognition.

▶ Write an essay entitled 'Real and Imaginary' in which you consider the following:
— evidence that this story is based on real people
— reasons why Alice Walker may have chosen to link the imaginary characters in this story with real people
— reasons why she chose to focus on the character of Gracie Mae Still rather than Traynor

— the way in which the story is written, particularly the style, structure and tone; how these add to its realism

— your opinions about what lies at the heart of the story.

▶ It is likely that after Traynor's death there would be a number of features on TV and radio and in newspapers and magazines about his life.

  a Imagine that Gracie Mae Still is being interviewed for such a feature. In pairs, discuss the questions she could be asked and the replies she may give; then, either act out the interview or write it up for the appropriate media.

  b Continue the story in the same style and write about the approaches made to Gracie Mae by the media, and her responses to them.

▶ 'Nineteen Fifty-Five' takes up a number of themes:
  — the record/music industry
  — stardom
  — relationships
  — song-writing
  Choose one of these themes and say what you learn about it from reading the story.

▶ What to call a story is always an important decision for a writer. Consider the title of this story and the reason Alice Walker may have had for choosing it. Then think of two or three alternative titles she could have used, giving reasons why you think they are suitable. Below are four titles you might like to comment on:
  'The Emperor of Rock and Roll'
  'Any Woman's Blues'
  'I ain't lived long enough'
  'Written by Gracie Mae Still'

▶ In 'Nineteen Fifty-Five' Alice Walker often places humour and suffering side by side in order to highlight the relationship between Gracie Mae and Traynor. Look in detail at the three sections beginning 'The boy's house is something else' (page 38), 'Gracie Mae, he says down the table' (page 38), and 'Traynor is all corseted down nice' (page 40). Discuss the juxtaposition of humour and pathos in these sections.

A Dangerous Influence

Before reading

▶ List three or four things which could be called 'dangerous influences'. Briefly discuss the ideas you have come up with. Is there a general agreement in your group or a wide range of opinions?

▶ Read the first few paragraphs of the story down to 'put it down to shyness' (page 44). Are there any clues in the story so far which help you predict what 'dangerous influence' this story may be about?

During reading

▶ Stop reading just over half-way through the story, after ' "Now we know why she keeps her hair so short", said Gloria solemnly, and always wears trousers." ' (page 51). At this point in the story, which characters do your sympathies lie with? Read to the end of the story. Have you changed your opinion?

After reading

▶ At the end of the story Miss Dangerfield goes home. Write the conversation she has with Lilian that evening.

▶ Short stories about sexuality are not usually included in anthologies for school and college students. What are your opinions on the inclusion of 'A Dangerous Influence' in this collection?

▶ Words have dictionary meanings but they also have connotations, and can be used hurtfully, as the reaction to Marcia's use of the word 'spinster' in the story shows. Using the examples given below and others you can think of, write about your opinions of sexist language and try to suggest ways in which it could be avoided.

Different meanings?
spinster — bachelor
mistress — master
governess — governor
Miss/Mrs — Mr

Male equivalents?
crumpet — ?
tart — ?
dish — ?
slag — ?

Alternatives?
man-made
manning (the shop)
man-power
man-to-man
fireman

Why doesn't the English language include words like these?
husband-swapping; chargentleman; woman-power; bit of trouser.

▶ ' "I am surprised to find that you do not seem to understand the way society works. In a community we have to think of other people. Whether you like it or not, you and your kind are a minority, and your — practices are simply not acceptable to the vast majority of people." ' (page 54)

Taken out of context this quotation could apply to a number of different groups of people: for example, ethnic minorities, youth groups, single parents, travellers/gypsies, lesbians and gays.

Write an essay in which you examine one or more of these different groups and argue the case for their right to live free from discrimination.

▶ Imagine that in her next job Lizzie is sacked because she is a lesbian, and she decides to take her employer to an industrial tribunal for unfair dismissal.
Either: Act out the tribunal hearing in which Lizzie, her union representative and her employer put their case, and a panel of arbitrators decide the outcome.
Or: Write out the speeches which Lizzie, her union representative and her employer would put forward at such a tribunal.

White Lies

| Before reading |

▶ What does the title of this story suggest it may be about? Think carefully about the different meanings it may have.

| During reading |

▶ While you are reading the story look out for the following lines:

'I think I resented him because he was new ... But he was not interested in my experiences. There was a great deal I could have told him.' (page 59)

'I heard a great fuss in the kitchen, Jerry telling Ameena not to do the ironing, Ameena protesting . . .' (page 61)

'She looked like a very dangerous fly which had buzzed into the room.' (page 62)

'I must admit that it gave me a certain pleasure . . . Jerry deserved to suffer . . . what I had told him had been true.' (page 68)

'As we chatted over the fence I heard Jerry's voice: *She's screaming for it.* I said, "We'll go horseback riding." ' (page 69)

'Everyone who knew Africa knew that.' (page 69).

What do these lines have in common with the story as a whole?

▶ Stop reading *after* the section ending, 'Jika was coughing and stirring the flames with a stick.' (page 64). In groups discuss Ameena's motives for visiting Jerry. Who do you agree with — Jerry or the narrator?

After reading

▶ Discuss all the reasons the author may have had for calling the story 'White Lies'. Consider its common meaning and also the connection it may have with the character and the setting. Write up the conclusions you have come to.

▶ Compare and contrast the characters of Jerry and the narrator. Which do you have more sympathy with by the end of the story? Do you consider that justice gets done in the end? You may find it helpful to look at the quotations above before you begin.

▶ Decide which of the following statements best sums up the story as a whole. Find examples from the story to back up your choice.
   This story is about ambition and pride.
   This story is about impatience and deceit.
   This story is about ignorance and superstition.
   This story is about success and failure.
   This story is about power and greed.
   Add some more statements of your own if you wish.

▶ Write a story of your own titled 'White Lies' which takes up the themes within this tale, but places the action in another setting.

▶ How does Paul Theroux emphasise both the humour and the unpleasantness of Jerry's sufferings from the maggots? Look closely at his style of writing.

▶ Women and men are presented in varying ways and with different attitudes in this story. What do you feel the author is saying about the sexes in 'White Lies'?

Coffee for the Road

Before reading

▶ Think of some occasions when you have wanted to do something you consider perfectly reasonable and have been prevented by those who have power or authority over you.
— What have these things been?
— What has your reaction been?
    After reading this story, discuss how *you* would have reacted in the situations described.

▶ What does the title of this story suggest it may be about?

▶ Read the opening paragraph and try to establish the country in which the story is set.

During reading

▶ Stop reading after the following points in the story and, based on what you have read, try to predict what may happen next:
— at the *end* of the paragraph beginning, 'The sun was a coppery smear . . .' (page 72)
— at the *end* of the paragraph beginning, 'Give me the flask . . .' (page 74)
— at the *end* of the paragraph beginning, 'The road speared once more . . .' (page 76).

▶ Write down the explicit and implicit references to racial prejudice in the story.

After reading

▶ Look again at the section of the story which starts with the words 'She opened the door and slid out' (page 74), and runs on to the paragraph ending 'The dark woman turned and stalked from the café in a rage' (page 76). Imagine you are adapting this story for television and are currently working on the shooting script for this scene.
    a Write the directions for the actors, including movements/actions, expressions, lines they speak, tone of voices.

   b Draw a diagram of the scene and describe in detail the props and the atmosphere you wish to create.

▶ The writer of this story builds up tension in a variety of ways. For example: contrasting the states of mind of the mother and her children; describing the people and the countryside the family drive past; setting the story in South Africa, thus drawing on our knowledge of social and political conditions in that country.

   Referring closely to the text, examine the build up of tension; use quotations to support the points you make.

▶ Continue the story and describe what happens when the woman and her children return to the town. Try, as far as possible, to write in the style of the original story.

▶ Write a story of your own which takes up some of the themes within this story and follows a similar structure.

Reunion

Before reading

▶ This story begins: 'People of Earth, do not be afraid. We come in peace — and why not? For we are your cousins; we have been here before'. Using the title and this opening paragraph, spend five minutes brainstorming ideas about what is going to happen in this story. Is there general agreement about what 'type' of story this may be — in other words, what 'genre' it may fit into?

During reading

▶ Try to work out who is speaking in the story.

▶ Stop reading at the *end* of the paragraph beginning, 'But two million years ago' (page 80). Discuss what kind of disease this could be and what effects it had had.

After reading

▶ Imagine that the story is a scene from a radio play or television film.
   a Write a script adapting it for the appropriate medium. Remember you will have to decide where the scene is taking place and which actors will be present.
   b Write another scene which takes place later on after the people in the space ship have landed.

▶ Discuss how the meaning and effect of the story change if the last line is removed. Make up some alternative last lines to 'Reunion'.

▶ What thematic links do you see between this story and others in the anthology?

A Lot to Learn

Before reading

▶ 'The Materializer was completed.'
'Chuckling, he experimented further.'
The first of these two sentences is the opening line of a short story; the second occurs about half-way through. The story is less than 200 words long! Incorporating the two sentences, write a story of your own of a similar length. When you have written your stories, read them out and compare them with others in your group. Are there many similarities in the type of stories which have been written, or are they quite different? Did the words 'Materializer' and 'experimented' lead some of you to write stories in a particular genre?

After reading

▶ Compare your stories with 'A Lot to Learn'.

Has this story given you any ideas for making improvements to your own? For example: changing the style and tone of your story; using short sentences; having the central character make a mistake; using a twist at the end? If you consider your stories are good enough make them into a collection, design a cover and give it a title. The collection could be given to other students.

True Romance

Before reading

▶ Thinking about what Jane Rogers writes on p. 90 and about different *types* of stories, can you identify where these two passages might have come from? What clues in each passage help you to decide?

'Ever since she'd started work in the office and John had become so friendly to her, there had been one thing on Sheila's mind: the office party. For weeks she'd been saving up her wages to buy a complete new outfit because she had to look dazzling enough for John to *really* notice her.'

'James Holborough had just completed yet another successful mission for CI5 but there was no time to waste on congratulations. Enemy agents had been identified in the heart of CI5 itself. Holborough's next task: to find out the identity of those involved and smash the spy ring forever.'

| During reading |

▶ This is a kind of two-in-one story; its design is rather unusual. Make a note of the contrasting stylistic features within the two tales.

| After reading |

▶ These two 'stories' use the same situations and characters but they have been written for different purposes and audiences. Choose any two paragraphs or sections and make a detailed comparison of their different styles and intentions. You could begin by looking at the use of adjectives, the length of sentences, the description of the characters' feelings.

Conclude by saying why you think the author of this story chose to write and structure it in the way she did; what points she was trying to get across to her readers; and why she chose this title.

▶ Look at a story or picture story in a magazine or comic aimed at girls or at boys, and write an alternative interpretation of the story. You could also do the same exercise for a problem page or horoscope.

▶ In pairs, take the two versions of 'First Kiss' (pages 84–86) and match up the parts of the story which directly correspond to each other.

For example: 'She looked forward to Sunday all week, and time passed so slowly it seemed more like a year. But like all good things, it proved a day well worth waiting for.'

This piece corresponds with: 'On Sunday we were supposed to be going for a walk.'

Then prepare a dramatic reading of the parts side by side, highlighting and perhaps satirising the differences between the two.

▶ From your reading of 'True Romance', 'Reunion' and 'A Lot to Learn' what ideas have you formed about different kinds of 'genre' writing?

Compile a list of the different 'fictional ingredients' you would expect to find in the following:

— science fiction story
— romance story
— detective/thriller story
— Western story
— travel story
— horror story

▶ Using 'True Romance' as a model, write your own two-in-one story.

The Story of an Hour

Before reading

▶ What does the title and the first paragraph of this story suggest it may be about?

▶ What constraints would the writer have to deal with because of the title she has chosen?

During reading

▶ Write down the points at which your expectations change or are challenged. Make a mental note of what you are expecting to happen as the story draws to its close.

After reading

▶ In pairs, discuss the following statements:
This story is about
— a woman's reaction to the death of her husband
— the constraints marriage puts on women and men
— the inability of people to show their true feelings
— the oppression of women
— what a sudden shock can do to someone with a weak heart.
Add more statements if you wish.
Choose the statements you agree with and write about your reasons for selecting them. Show what you have written to at least one other person, discuss it with them and make any necessary changes. Use what you have written so far, together with the notes you made during reading, as the basis for a critical piece of writing about the story.

▶ 'When the doctors came they said she had died of heart disease — of joy that kills' (page 93).

Explain the meaning of this sentence.

Do you think it makes an effective ending to the story? What effect does it have on the story as a whole?

▶ Write a story of your own in which the time covered is approximately one hour.

You may find the following titles useful:

'The Hour before Dawn'
'A Journey'
'The Lunch-hour'
'Brief Encounter'
'The Longest Hour'
'At the Launderette'
'The Rush-hour'
'The Delay'

Samphire

| Before reading |

▶ 'Sheer, sheer, the white cliff rising, straight up from the sea'. This opening phrase has an obvious drama to it, once you have read the story. What ideas or 'echoes' does it offer before you read any further?

▶ Have you been involved in a moment of high drama — perhaps an accident — with someone you know well? What were your feelings and thoughts at the time, and afterwards?

| During reading |

▶ Stop reading after each break in the text and, based on what you have read thus far, try to predict what may happen next.

Note: In the second section the man and woman return to the cliff to look at the clump of samphire again, so amongst other things you need to decide:

— who wanted to make the return journey

— what happens during the journey and when they reach the cliff.

▶ Decide the answers to the following questions:

— how long have the man and woman known each other?

— why have they decided to come to this place?

▶ Write a conversation between Lacey and a friend which takes place after the couple have returned home, where Lacey describes what happened on their holiday.

▶ Write a conversation between the hotel-keeper and a hotel guest in which they discuss their impressions of Molly and Lacey.

▶ In this story it is Lacey who does all the talking. The author has decided not to let Molly speak. Why might this be? What does the story gain or lose because of this?

▶ It is only towards the end of the story that we begin to understand Molly's feelings and the reasons which drove her to attempt what she did. In your own words retell the whole story as a first-person monologue from Molly's point of view. If you wish, you could write it in the form of a 'flashback' in which she retraces the events which drove her on.

▶ Write an additional piece — either in the form of a playscript or a short story — which begins where Patrick O'Brian leaves us.

▶ Pick out four or five phrases or sentences which strike you as particularly effective; explain their meaning in the context of the plot and say how they add to the overall meaning of the story. Here are four examples you could use:
   — 'There was something in her throat so strong that she could not have spoken if it had been for her life.'
   — 'The extreme of horror on it, too.'
   — 'He had fallen off a cliff all right.'
   — 'her dying face'

Sumitra

▶ This is an adaptation from a novel called *Sumitra's Story*. It is about Sumitra Patel, a Ugandan Asian, and her family who were forced to flee from President Amin's reign of terror in the 1970s, and come to live in London. They have now been living in London for five years.

The characters in this story are:

The Patel family

Mai, mother	Gopal	
Bap, father	Motiben	
Sumitra, aged 16 ⎤	Leela	⎫
Sandya, aged 14 ⎪	Jayant	⎬ relatives
Bimla, aged 10 ⎬ daughters	Trupti	⎪
Ela, aged 8 ⎦		⎭

Maria, a young white woman Sumitra first met when they were both living in temporary homeless family accommodation.
Sally, her daughter.
Martin, a teacher who has recently married Maria.

▶ Discuss your own experiences of and reading about people's feelings and problems when moving from one country to another, or from one culture into another.

During reading

▶ Make notes on Sumitra's changing feelings in this story.

After reading

▶ Write three entries in Sumitra's diary:
— on the day the story opens
— on the day of the trip to the seaside
— on the day of Bimla's party.

▶ Make notes on the attitudes expressed by the following characters to marriage:
Sumitra
Mai
Maria
Jayant
Compare these attitudes to those put forward in 'The Story of an Hour' and Samphire'.

▶ Mai talks about 'the British tradition in which they lived'. Discuss *a* what Mai means when she says this; *b* what British tradition means to you and other members of your group.

▶ 'It was funny how different things seemed. Yesterday everything was difficult and dreary. Now, nothing seemed the same. It was a matter of perspective' (page 105).

Write a story of your own based on this quotation.

▶ This story touches on a number of issues:
— maintaining cultural traditions
— racism in society and schools
— the generation gap
— the importance of education.

What are your own views on these subjects? You may wish to mount a formal debate in your group on one of these.

The Sniper

| Before reading |

▶ What does the title of this story suggest it may be about?

▶ Read the introduction on page 109 very carefully. It helps us understand the action of the story and places the fighting in its historical context. You might like to find out more about this period in Irish history.

| During reading |

▶ Try to build up a visual picture or image of the street in which the story takes place so that you could draw a diagram of it.

▶ Make a note of the various stylistic devices — short sentences and 'action' words — which the writer uses.

| After reading |

▶ Do you feel that this story is intended to make you consider the horrors of civil war or family tragedy — or both?

▶ What details in the story suggest that the Republican sniper has much experience of the kind of situation he finds himself in?

▶ Draw a plan of the scene in which the story takes place. Using it and other clues you can find in the story, explain in your own words how this tragedy may have occurred.

▶ In his desire to find out the identity of the man he has killed, the Republican exposes himself to great danger. Re-read the last few paragraphs of the story, and then continue the story so that the reader finds out what happens next. Try as far as possible to write in the style of the original text; pay particular attention to length of sentences and paragraphs.

▶ Write a short newspaper report covering the personal tragedy of this event and setting it against the background of fighting in Ireland at the time.

▶ Write your own story set against a background of political unrest. You could find ideas and information for such a story by looking at newspaper reports.

Meeting in Milkmarket

Before reading

▶ Think back to your primary school — to someone you knew then and who you have not seen since. If you met them now what would you have to say to them? What questions would you ask?

▶ Look at these opening phrases of paragraphs in 'Meeting in Milk-market' and try to predict what the story may be about:
— 'Thirty-five years ago. . .'
— 'Today I met. . .'
— 'I remember. . .'
— 'I find it now very difficult to say. . .'
— 'Today. . .'
— 'But what I cannot understand is. . .'.

During reading

▶ Pay particular attention to the memories the narrator has about George:
— at their first meeting
— of the way their friendship was established
— of the things George liked to do
— of what caused them to lose touch with each other.

After reading

▶ In pairs, look at the following statements. Decide which best describe what this story is about. Add more of your own if necessary.

Follow On **147**

This story is about:
— a brief encounter between two old friends
— the divisions brought about by social class
— the living conditions in parts of Barbados
— the real facts of life
— nostalgia for the innocence of childhood.

▶ 'The true facts of life are hardly so simple. The mating of male and female . . . these . . . hold less mystery and need far less explanation than the conventions and artificialities which we have erected to separate one person from another' (page 117).

Discuss the meaning of this quotation with reference to the story and to the wider implications it has for the way society is organised.

▶ Re-read the last two paragraphs of the story, paying particular attention to George's attitude to the meeting. Write a story in a similar style which describes the feelings and memories which are evoked here by John Wickham.

Happy Birthday

Before reading

▶ Write down the following names of characters whom Ollie comes across during the story. Make this into a sort of chart, leaving yourself enough room to write down notes about each:
Granddaddy
Chalky
Wilma
the cooks
kids to play ball with
Mrs Robinson
Ronnie
the big boys

During reading

▶ Write down the ways in which Ollie tries to amuse herself during her birthday and the reasons she is unsuccessful.

After reading

▶ Did this story make you:

— want to laugh?
— feel sorry for Ollie?
— do both?
— remember similar situations yourself?
   Why do you think the author decided to write the story?
   Was she trying to say something in particular?

▶ Re-tell part or all of the story as a first-person narrative from Ollie's point of view, trying as far as possible to write in the style of the original.

▶ Continue the story in the same style as Toni Cade Bambara, and write about what happens to Ollie when she returns home. Make use of the notes that you have drafted out about the characters.

Meeting in Milkmarket and Happy Birthday

Comparisons
Both these stories could be describing real experiences; both are written in very different ways. For example:

Milkmarket
first-person narrative
flashback
descriptive/reflective/lyrical
mainly narrative
from an adult viewpoint
a definite author's voice, drawing the reader's attention to certain
   points

Happy Birthday
third-person narrative
chronological
snappy/dialect/short sentences
mixture of narrative and dialogue
from a child's viewpoint
'a day in the life of', leaving the reader to draw her/his own conclusions

▶ Write an essay comparing the two approaches to writing about real events.

▶ Choose one style and write about an incident in your own life — in other words, a piece of autobiography.

Experimenting with style and form

▶ In 'Happy Birthday' the 'friendship' between Ollie and Wilma is described. Write a story similar to 'Meeting in Milkmarket' in which the two meet again many years later.

▶ Take one of the incidents described in 'Meeting in Milkmarket'. Write a full story about it, in a similar style to 'Happy Birthday', as if it were happening in the present.

Further ideas for group and individual work

▶ As well as telling a story, writers often want to make us think deeply about an idea or theme or issue. Make a list of the various themes raised in this collection. Which themes do the stories have in common? Have any of the stories made you rethink your opinions or beliefs?

▶ Which characters in the stories did you enjoy reading about or even identify with? Write your own story centring on one of these characters, or bring together characters from different stories — for example, Tracey in 'Pin Money' and Lizzie in 'A Dangerous Influence'.

▶ What are your reactions to the ways in which the stories end? Look closely at the closing lines of each story. If you find the ending unsatisfactory, try rewriting — or acting out — an alternative one.

▶ Some of these stories offer humour to the reader. Look back over the stories and attempt to analyse writers' use of comedy. You could consider 'Nineteen Fifty-Five', 'White Lies', 'A Lot to Learn' and 'Happy Birthday'.

▶ 'Meeting in Milkmarket' uses the first-person 'I' narrator to tell the story, while 'The Sniper' has a third-person narrator observing the action from outside. Which type of narrator is used in each of the fourteen tales? 'True Romance' is a particularly interesting example to look at.

  What seem to you the advantages and disadvantages of the different types of narrative standpoint? Rewrite any of the stories, changing the narrator's point of view.

▶ When people write fiction they often do so based on something they have actually seen or done themselves. Which of these stories seems to you in any way autobiographical? What clues do you look for? Re-read what some of the writers themselves say about their stories on pages 27, 42, 79, 90, 98–99, 108 and 119.

▶ Why does someone behave in the way they do? What causes them to take one line of action rather than another? What motivates the characters in these stories? Working in groups, choose one of the stories. Then take it in turns to play the part of one of the characters. Each character is placed in the witness-box and quizzed by the others as to why they behaved as they did in the story. You might start with 'Coffee for the Road' or 'A Dangerous Influence'.

▶ Mount a dramatised reading — complete with sound effects and music — of one of the stories. This is best practised in small groups and then presented to a larger audience.

▶ 'In writing the short story it is the lines that are left out that are of paramount importance . . . The short story must depict more by implication than by statement, more by what is left out than left in. It ought, in fact, to resemble lace: strong but delicate, deviously woven yet full of light and air.' These lines were written by the great short-storyteller H.E. Bates. Think back over the stories in this collection and discuss whether the above comments ring true. You will need to look closely at the style of individual writers.

▶ 'A first reading makes you want to know what will happen; a second makes you understand why it happens; a third makes you think'. How true is this in your reading and re-reading of the stories in *It's Now or Never*?

▶ Why do you think the editors of this collection of short stories decided to give it the title *It's Now or Never*? Does it represent a unifying theme? Does it have wider connotations? Can you think of a better title?

Writing a review

Which of the stories did you enjoy most? Write a short review of your favourite story from this collection which will make other students want to read it. The plan below offers some starting-points.

Setting

Where and when is the story set?
Does this affect how the characters behave and what they do?

Is there a special mood or atmosphere to the story?

Plot

How does the story begin?
What is the story about?
Are the events ordinary and everyday — or *extra*ordinary?
Do the scenes follow on from one another — or is there a flashback?
Where are the climaxes?
How does the story end? Is everything explained or are you left guessing?

Characters

Who are the main characters?
What are they like? — sex, age, nationality, strengths and weaknesses, behaviour, etc.
Do you find them interesting?
Do you take sides with any of them?
Do they face a problem? Do they solve it?

Style

Who is telling the story? First or third-person narrator?
Are there any special effects used?
How is dialogue used?
Are there lots of long descriptions?
Is there humour or suspense?

Themes

What reason do you think the author had for telling this particular story? Are there any special messages or ideas?

General

Did you enjoy the story?
Did you learn anything from it? Has it changed your attitudes about anything?
How did you feel during and after reading it — excited, tense, annoyed, amused?
Will you look for other stories by the same writer? Why?
Would you recommend it to other students?

Writing your own short story

▶ Plan out your own story by asking and answering the following questions:
— What is going to be the *subject* of the story?
— Where is it going to take place? Are there going to be several different places?
— How many characters are there going to be?
— Are you going to use first or third-person narration?
— Are there any particular ideas or themes you want to put across to your reader?
— Are you going to have dialogue, detailed descriptions, dialect, humour, suspense, or what?

▶ Think about your *audience*. Ask yourself the question: *Who* am I writing for?

▶ A plan for writing:
— Jot down your ideas for the story.
— Sort out roughly how many paragraphs you'll need. How long will the story be?
— Write a first draft of your story. Redraft if necessary.
— Ask somebody to read it through with you. How would they make it better?
— Rewrite your final version, paying particular attention to spelling, sentences, paragraphs and appropriateness of language.
— Read it over once more to see that you haven't made any basic errors.

Note

If you have views on any aspects of the collection, the editors would like to hear from you. Write c/o Bell & Hyman, Denmark House, 37–39 Queen Elizabeth Street, London SE1 2QB.

Further Reading

Note: Where a book is published in both hardback and paperback editions, details of paperback only are given.

Pin Money

This story by **Jennifer Gubb** was first published in a collection titled *The Open Road* (Onlywomen Press) in which the writer's main concerns are with country life and women growing up in this environment.
Related reading:

Tough Annie by Annie Barnes, Stepney Books (1980)
Women and the Wire — about the Greenham Common Women — B. Harford and B. Hopkins, Sisterwrite (1984)
My Song is My Own, a book of song lyrics, Pluto Press (1979)
The Laundry Girls, a play by Bill Owen, Dramascripts, Macmillan Educational (1973)
These Boots Were Made For Walking, a play by Bill Owen, Dramascripts, Macmillan Educational (1980)
Rosie the Riveter, film/video available from ILEA Central Library

Nineteen Fifty-Five

This story is taken from a powerful collection titled *You Can't Keep a Good Woman Down* (The Women's Press). The American writer **Alice Walker** has also published another short-story collection *In Love and Trouble,* and the novel *The Color Purple* (The Women's Press).

Readers might also like to read Buchi Emecheta's novels *Second Class Citizen* and *Double Yoke* (Fontana).

Similar themes may be taken up in:

Black Lives, White Worlds, Keith Ajegbo, Cambridge University Press (1982)
I Know Why the Caged Bird Sings, Maya Angelou, Virago (1984)
A Measure of Time, Rosa Guy, Virago (1984)
Roots, Alex Haley, Picador (1978)
The Autobiography of Malcolm X, Penguin (1970)

A Dangerous Influence

Lucy Whitman has also written 'The Severed Tongue', included in an anthology of short stories entitled *Girls Next Door: Lesbian Feminist Stories* (The Women's Press).

Related reading:

Dance on My Grave, Aidan Chambers, Bodley Head (1982)
Who Lies Inside, Timothy Ireland, Gay Men's Press (1984)
The Handbook of Non-Sexist Writing, Casey Miller and Kate Swift, The Women's Press (1981)
Faultline, Sheila Ortiz Taylor, The Women's Press (1982)
Inside the Winter Gardens, David Rees (1984)
In the Tent, David Rees, Dobson Books (1979)
Love Stories by New Women, (eds) Charleen Swansea and Barbara Kuhn Campbell, The Women's Press (1979)
Something To Tell You, (ed.) Lorraine Trenchard and Hugh Warren, London Gay Teenage Group (1984)
Two's Company, Catherine Storr, Patrick Hardy Books (1984)
Hetero, Homo, Bi or Nothing — essay by Robert Westall in *Is Anyone There?*, (ed.) Sutcliffe, Penguin (out of print)

White Lies

This story by **Paul Theroux** first appeared in a volume titled *World's End* (Penguin). *Sinning With Annie* (Hamish Hamilton), is another collection of stories by the same author; perhaps his best-known novels are *Saint Jack* and *The Great Railway Bazaar* (Penguin).

The Longman Drumbeat series has an interesting selection of writings about Africa, including *Muriel at Metropolitan* by Miriam Tlali and *Violence* by Festus Iyayi.

Coffee for the Road

Other stories by **Alex La Guma** are collected in *A Walk in the Night*, Heinemann African Writers Series.

Related reading:
Jail Diary of Albie Sachs, David Edgar, Collings (1978)
'Sizwe Bansi is Dead' in *Statements* by Athol Fugard, Oxford University Press (1974)
Selected Stories, Nadine Gordimer, Penguin (1983)
In the Castle of My Skin, George Lamming, Longman Drumbeat Series (1979)
To Kill a Mockingbird, Harper Lee, Pan (1974)
The Grass is Singing, Doris Lessing, Panther (1980)
A Taste of Freedom, Julius Lester, Longman Knockouts Series (1983)
Bandiet: Seven Years in a South African Prison, Hugh Lewin, Heinemann African Writers Series (1982)
Debbie Go Home, Alan Paton, Penguin (1965)
Roll of Thunder, Hear My Cry, Mildred Taylor, Penguin (1980)

Reunion

Arthur C. Clarke has been one of the greatest and most prolific science-fiction writers; his work includes countless short stories, collections include *2001* (Inner Circle Books), *2010* (Granada), *Of Time and Stars* (Penguin) and *Wind from the Sun* (Pan).

Further examples of the science fiction genre:

Antigrat, Nicholas Fisk, Puffin (1982); *On the Flip Side*, Kestrel, (1983)
Science Fiction, John L. Foster (ed.), John Murray (1978)
Science Fiction, James Gibson (ed.), Ward Lock (1975)
13 Science Fiction Stories, Paul Groves and Nigel Grimshaw, Edward Arnold (1979)
Alien Worlds, (1982); *Day of the Starwind*, (1982), *Galactic Warlord*, (1980), *Planet of the Warlord* (1982), etc., Douglas Hill, Piccolo

A Lot to Learn

This story by **R. T. Kurosaka** is published in a collection called *Twisters* (ed.) Steve Bowles, Collins.

It is interesting to draw a distinction between science-fiction and science-fantasy: between what might be possible in the future and what is pure fantasy.

Recommended reading:

Isaac Asimov: *The Naked Sun, The Gods Themselves*, and *The End of Eternity* are recommended novels. His short stories are available in *The Early Asimov*, Volumes 1, 2, 3.

Ray Bradbury: *The Martian Chronicles, Fahrenheit 451* and *The Small Assassin* are recommended novels. *The Illustrated Man* includes some of his best short stories.

All the above are published by Panther.

True Romance

This story was first published in the feminist magazine 'Spare Rib'. **Jane Rogers** has written two novels: *Separate Tracks*, and *Her Living Image* (Faber).

Other recommended reading:

The Gender Trap, Carol Adams and Rae Laurikietis, Virago (1976)
Selling Pictures, teaching pack, British Film Institute (1983)
Gregory's Girl in 'Act Now' series, Cambridge University Press, (1983)
Girls are Powerful: Young Women's Writings from Spare Rib, (ed.) Susan Hemmings, Sheba (1982)
Comics and Magazines and *The English Curriculum: Gender*, ILEA English Centre (1985)
First Love, Last Rights, Ian McEwan, Cape (1975)
S.W.A.L.K., Paula Milne, Thames-Methuen (1983)

The Story of an Hour

This story was first published in *Portraits* (The Women's Press). **Kate Chopin** wrote many similar stories about the role and repression of women in the latter years of the nineteenth century. At the time of writing, her stories were much criticized for their explicit and daring scenes, and treatment of controversial issues. Her novel *The Awakening* is well worth reading (also published by The Women's Press).

Further stories about women's lives can be found in:

Unwinding Threads: Writing by Women in Africa, selected and edited by Charlotte H. Bruner, Heinemann African Writers Series (1985)
Selected Stories, Nadine Gordimer, Penguin (1983)
The Women of Brewster Place, Gloria Naylor, Sphere Books (1984)
The Penguin Dorothy Parker, Penguin (1977)

Samphire

Patrick O'Brian is best known for his series of novels featuring Jack Aubrey and Doctor Stephen Maturin: *Master and Commander* (Fontana), *HMS Surprise* (Fontana), *The Mauritius Command* (Collins) and *Desolation Island* (Fontana).

Novels and stories which explore similar themes:

A Roald Dahl Selection, (ed.) Roy Blatchford, Longman Imprint Books (1980)

The Charlotte Perkins Gilman Reader, Charlotte Gilman, The Women's Press (1981)

Meetings and Partings, (ed.) M. Marland, Longman Imprint Books (1984)

Sumitra

Rukshana Smith is an Asian writer who has also published *Rainbows of the Gutter* (Bodley Head).

Other related reading:

Poona Company, Farrukh Dhondy, Gollancz (1980)

Our Lives, ILEA English Centre (1979)

The Woman Warrior, Maxine Hong Kingston, Picador (1981)

It's My Life, Robert Leeson, Armada Lions (1981)

The Lonely Londoners, Samuel Selvon, Longman Drumbeat Series (1979)

Breaking the Silence, (ed.) J. Walters and M. Burbidge, Centreprise Books (1981)

Finding A Voice, Amrit Wilson, Virago (1978)

The Sniper

Other books by **Liam O'Flaherty** include: *The Pedlar's Revenge and other stories, Selected Short Stories* (New English Library), *The Wave and other stories* (Longman Imprint Books).

Irish authors have distinguished themselves as short-storytellers; among those worth reading further are:

Dubliners, James Joyce, Penguin (1984)

A Scandalous Woman and other stories, Edna O'Brien, Penguin (1976)

My Oedipus Complex, Frank O'Connor, Penguin (1984)

Daughters of Passion, Julia O'Faolain, Penguin (1982)

Collected Stories, Sean O'Faolain, Penguin (1982)

Across the Barricades, by Joan Lingard (Puffin) is set in Northern Ireland in recent years and covers the poignant tragedies of civil war. *This Way for the Gas, Ladies and Gentlemen*, Tadeusz Borowski, Penguin (1976), offers some horrifying accounts of life in the Jewish prisoner-of-war camps during the Second World War. *Talking in Whispers*, James Watson (Collins), is a thriller set in Chile.

Meeting in Milkmarket

John Wickham is a Barbadian writer. His compilation *West Indian Stories*, Ward Lock Educational, includes some of his short stories. Also recommended:

> *Come to Mecca*, Farrukh Dhondy, Collins (1978) – particularly the story 'Free Dinners'
> *Caribbean Stories*, (ed.) Michael Marland, Longman Imprint Books (1978)
> *Brown Girl, Brownstones*, Paule Marshall, Virago (1982)
> *Song of Solomon*, Toni Morrison, Panther (1980)
> *Ways of Sunlight*, Samuel Selvon, Longman Drumbeat Series (1979)
> *Best West Indian Stories*, Kenneth Ramchand, Nelson Carribean (1982)

Happy Birthday

This story is available in *Gorilla, My Love* by **Toni Cade Bambara**, The Women's Press. She has also written *The Seabirds are Still Alive* (more short stories) and *The Salt Eaters*, both published by The Women's Press.

Related reading:

The Friends, Rosa Guy, Puffin (1977)
Edith Jackson, Rosa Guy, Puffin (1985)
Over our Way, (ed.) Jean D'Costa and Velma Pollard, Longman Caribbean (1980)

Other recommended volumes of short stories:

A Quiver Full of Arrows, Jeffrey Archer, Coronet (1982)
Short Stories from India, Pakistan and Bangladesh, (ed.) Ranjana Ash, Harrap (1980)
The Human Element, Stan Barstow, Longman Imprint Books (1970)
The Stories of John Cheever, Penguin (1982)
Chekhov: The Early Stories, Abacus–Sphere (1984)
Modern Short Stories 2, (ed.) Giles Gordon, Dent (1982)
The Shout and other stories, Robert Graves, Penguin (1978)
Collected Stories, Graham Greene, Penguin (1970)
A Bit of Singing and Dancing, Susan Hill, Penguin (1976)
Metamorphosis and other stories, Franz Kafka, Penguin (1970)
A Life of Her Own, Maeve Kelly, Poolbeg Press (1976)
Collected stories of Somerset Maugham, Pan (1976)
Selected Short Stories, Guy de Maupassant, Penguin (1971)
Stories of the Waterfront, John Morrison, Penguin (1984)
The Penguin Complete Saki, Penguin (1982)
Vintage Thurber (Vols 1 and 2), Penguin (1983)
Watching Me, Watching You, Fay Weldon, Coronet (1982)

Acknowledgements

The editors and publishers wish to thank the following for permission to reprint the short stories:

Onlywomen Press for 'Pin Money' by Jennifer Gubb, originally published in *The Open Road and Other Stories* (1983). Story note © Jennifer Gubb 1985.

The Women's Press for 'Nineteen Fifty-Five' by Alice Walker, originally published in *You Can't Keep a Good Woman Down* (1982). Story note © Alice Walker 1985.

Lucy Whitman for 'A Dangerous Influence' originally published in *Everday Matters: New Short Stories by Women*, Vol. 1, Sheba Feminist Publishers (1982).

Gillon Aitken for 'White Lies' by Paul Theroux, originally published in *World's End*, Hamish Hamilton (1980).

Tessa Sayle Literary & Dramatic Agency for 'Coffee for the Road' by Alex La Guma, originally published in *Modern African Stories*, Faber & Faber (1977). Story note © Alex La Guma 1985.

David Higham Associates Ltd for 'The Reunion' by Arthur C. Clarke, originally published in *The Wind from the Sun*, Gollancz (1972).

A.D. Peters & Co. Ltd for 'True Romance', originally titled 'The Real Thing' and published in 'Spare Rib', December 1978. Story note © Jane Rogers 1985.

Richard Scott Simon Ltd for 'Samphire' by Patrick O'Brian, originally published in 'Harper's Bazaar' (1953), from the collection *The Chian Wine*, Collins. Story note © Patrick O'Brian 1985.

The Bodley Head for 'Sumitra' by Rukshana Smith, an extract from *Sumitra's Story* (1982). Story note © Rukshana Smith 1985.

The Estate of Liam O'Flaherty for 'The Sniper' originally published in *The Short Stories of Liam O'Flaherty*, Cape (1937).

John Wickham for 'Meeting in Milkmarket'. Story note © John Wickham 1985.

Scott, Foresman and Company for 'Happy Birthday' by Toni Cade Bambara, originally published in *What's Happening* © 1969 Scott Foresman and Company.

The song 'Maintenance Engineer' © Sandra Kerr 1979, was originally published in *My Song Is My Own* © Frankie Armstrong, Kathy Henderson, Sandra Kerr, Alison McMorland, Pluto Press (1979).